WAR THUG

HUGO NAVIKOV

SEVERED PRESS
HOBART TASMANIA

WAR THUG

Copyright © 2016 by Severed Press

WWW.SEVEREDPRESS.COM

ISBN: 978-1-925493-04-7

WAR THUG

We called him Sarge, or sir. He had a name, of course, but in the years our SEAL unit was together, all of us grunts saw him as larger than life, more than any one name could describe. He was a force of nature. Sometimes, when we were in our sacks tethered to the bulkhead to keep us from floating around the transport ship, but not wanting to sleep yet, we referred to him (between ourselves only, in whispers) by the name he had tattooed on his massive arms, one word on each side:

"War" and "Thug." He was the War Thug.

None of us knew where he got that name, or why he had it carved into his body, but it described our platoon commander perfectly. He lived for war, and when serving with him, so did we. In my five tours of bouncing from planetary conflict to bug hunt to tech grab to just plain elimination of suspected alien terrorist cells, we never lost a SEAL. Our squad of 12 Space/Earth Atmosphere Leapers—you'll see in a minute why we SEALs have that designation—was the best in the business, and that was because of Sarge, our War Thug.

Funny thing was, he wasn't a sergeant at all—the Space Navy doesn't have that rank. We figured he was probably a Master Chief Petty Officer, the highest enlisted rank in our arm of the Space Service, an E-9, basically the same as a Sergeant Major in the other branches, many levels above a platoon sergeant. But we never knew for sure, because his arms were too big, too powerful, to fit into a regulation uniform, and his custom rags were without rank insignia. Sarge said we didn't need stripes anyway to tell us who listens to who when the fighting starts. He said if we didn't trust him—or if he lacked full faith he was in charge and knew what he was doing—then we were all gonna die on some godforsaken rock far from home, trying to take down the targets before they snuffed us. (And failing.) So we trusted him, and he trusted us. And that's what kept us all alive and a pack of ravening wolves behind our Alpha, who showed us what to kill, and even after all these tours, did it himself whenever he could.

War Thug ruined us for civilian life. I don't even know what I would do on Terra or any of the civilian colonies we're so often called upon to act as pest control. But the detail we were called to three years ago was the killing of an entire hive of bugs. We leapt onto the massive "space elevator" cord and fell to terminal velocity to get our boots on the ground of the largest moon of the largest gas giant orbiting Vega, Kokytos. The moon itself had a relatively thick atmosphere and both bodies had some official alphanumeric name none of us ever used. To us, the moon was immediately renamed Gale, not for some sweetheart back home, but for the hurricane-speed gusts created by gravitational forces between the moon and its tremendous planet. Gale was tidally locked with its gas-striped host, and if we could have waited a million years or so, our problem with it would be taken care of when the moon's orbit decayed enough to let it crash through the clouds and be destroyed.

However, the government of Terra needed this issue resolved in its favor *now*. Our home planet was still known as *Earth* among both residents and stellar colonists, but Sarge made us refer to it— if we referred to it at all, which was discouraged—as *Terra*. This, he said, was to help break bonds with our former home so we could keep our minds on the job ahead, not get wistful about the remainder of the planet we were fighting to keep safe.

Sarge made it clear that if we didn't do our job, and do it well, then Terra would fall to insectoid or worse invaders one day. This, he said, would be even more destructive than the war that was finally ended when the Space Navy was conceived. Soldiers (sailors, technically) were trained, Enhanced, and sent to wipe out the aggressor's planet until they left ours. They did retreat at last, after killing more than 75 percent of Earth's population but suffering even greater losses in our all-out counterattack on their rock. After the invaders were gone and back on their planet, we dropped a Super-Nuke on them and killed every single living thing anywhere upon or under its forever-ruined surface. I had never seen a Super-Nuke deployed or even heard of its use in the present day, and immersion vids during training showed me that I would never want to. Some said there was no such thing as a Super-Nuke, it being just a legend created to put Terrans at ease that we can kill entire populations of aggressive planets in one shot. But whatever they used, Super-Nuke or something else, we killed just about everything on the attackers' home world, and we killed the ones who fled from Terra. That was the beginning of the War Against Alien Aggression.

That Terran war had raged and ended before any of us grunts— or even Sarge, most likely—had been born. But we knew that if we didn't kill every alien son of a bitch we could, steal every bit of their technology, or in some cases just kill the bugs infesting a planet or moon so they wouldn't evolve into a threat, we might as well kiss humanity goodbye. Because it would happen again. We had to move "pro-actively," as the War Council had our teachers call it: Offensive conflicts that we would start and we would control; aggression instead of waiting for victimhood. The War Council was built on the philosophy of "kill them before they can kill us."

I want to tell you about the fight on Gale so you can understand what happened later, on our very next mission.

Going into the battle on Vega's giant moon, War Thug told us he would be proud of us grunts that day, whether we survived or not. But he added that he would be proud of *himself* only if we were in and out without losing a soldier *and* we eliminated the enemy entirely.

"You'll be proud, sir!" we all shouted in unison as we assembled and suited up in our heavy equipment. For once, we were thankful for the weight of the gear, since the gravity on Gale was less than one Terran G and the wind gusts were going to be stronger than anything something of human weight could usually endure and not be swept away.

Sarge smiled—he wasn't perpetually grim—and shouted his response: *"Damn right, I will!* Now you babies get your thumbs out of your mouths and *drop!"*

***

A "space elevator" isn't an elevator at all—it's a nigh-indestructible cable connecting a ship in geosynchronous orbit above the target spot on the surface of a planet or moon. The first soldier to drop guided the cable most of the way to the surface, releasing it and hitting his own chute (for drops onto planets with atmospheres—gas jets were used for thin or non-existent atmospheres) only after selecting the precise spot where its base would best penetrate the surface. Upon impact, the space elevator's base shot out root-like anchors that dig deep enough to keep the cable connected between the surface and the ship above in its stationary orbit around the planet's equator.

Geared up, we needed only to breathe calmly and attach our clips to our assigned spot on the rotator that would be feeding out the thousands of miles of foot-thick carbon-nanotube cable. Our tech guy and Drop Specialist, Leonard, got the elevator anchors secured on the surface and then gave the all-clear for us to join him.

As we did on every mission into whatever hellhole the Terran authorities sent us, we lined up and waited for the signal that the elevator had been successfully anchored. Once we got that signal, our clips—with us attached—shot out of the ship, following the now-anchored line all the way down to the surface.

Us twelve grunts leaped in order, as always, with Sarge bringing up the rear in case things went FUBAR and he needed to haul us back in. We leaped in reverse alphabetical order. Sarge had let us use our own names if they fit, but gave the rest of us nicknames to fit his alphabet scheme of keeping track of his grunts:

1. **Leonard:** Tech soldier. He was a handsome black kid who, for some reason, signed up with the Space Navy and found himself Enhanced to operate as a Faraday conductor cage. His right arm was lost as an infantryman before he joined our Enhanced crew, and his ability to magnify electric discharges was greatly increased by his automail prosthetic arm. Composed of an iron-silver alloy for maximum electrical conductivity and strength, the artificial arm allowed him to practically pull lightning from the sky and discharge it wherever he chose with his already-Enhanced body. The fake arm, like all modern prosthetics, fully connected with the motor and tactile nerves in his shoulder, as well as the muscles and sinew that grew into and around it, and it functioned as a normal arm and hand. Leonard was also our all-around technician who not only carried a SEAL railgun, but also knew exactly how they worked and how to repair one in the field. He worked closely with Inman, our ordnance man.

2. **Killshot:** Sniper. He was short and snakelike, perfect for allowing him to secure himself into tight spaces with his long-range photon rifle. The only thing that put down more alien bugs than Killshot was a neutron concussion grenade. His eyes were Enhanced, his optic nerves running through an electronic "cleanse" that allowed him to see the battlefield in visible, infrared, and ultraviolet wavelengths.

3. **Junebug:** Infantry. Maybe Sarge was a little old-school sexist, but he gave the female members of the platoon cuter names than the men. But while "Junebug" had an adorable name, she was an ox of a soldier—and that is definitely a compliment. Enhanced for density, she was broader in shoulder than some of the men in our platoon. She would barrel right through the mayhem if she saw a place to shove her beloved entrenching tool right through some bug's disgusting thorax, or sometimes just to knock a bunch of aliens to the ground and take them out one by one with fists, melee weapons, or even her railgun. She used her guns and rifles a lot, but there was no denying that she greatly preferred to feel nano-reinforced iron puncturing and then slashing through metal, flesh, exoskeleton, gelid ice armor, you name it.

4. **Inman:** Armor specialist. Also our ordnance expert. (Funny how those work so well together.) He knew what shell to use when as well as when it was time to go neutron or even nuclear. We had never been on such a losing end that we

had to use a Super-Nuke that would wipe out every living thing on a planet and good thing, too, because we were usually fighting bugs for planetary resources when we weren't launching a pre-emptive strike on sentient aliens to bring them into submission, and the Super-Nuke would just destroy *everything*. But even with the much less powerful tactical nuclear bomb, Sarge would never let Inman "nuke it from orbit," saying it wasn't warfare that way. He made sure we repaired to a safe distance, but close enough to feel the heat and the wind from the mushroom cloud as we erased our enemies in an endgame last resort. Inman had enhanced hearing, which helped him greatly when he needed to know how many bugs were coming and whether we needed to wipe them all out in one blow.

5. **Hog:** Infantry. A huge baby-faced farm boy who liked nothing more than running right at the enemy and scaring them. Then he killed them and ran to do it again. Completely fearless, or possibly just too dense to be afraid. Hog's Enhancement was a modest one, but every second he used it during battle was a bad thing for our enemy: he could, at will, make his entire body (and along with it anything he wore or held) vibrate at such a frequency that anything that touched him—or that he touched—would rattle in sympathetic vibration until it literally shook itself to death. (Or, in the case of machines, shook itself into its component pieces, which is what ended the existence of Hog's living targets as well.)

6. **Gunner:** Our gunnery sergeant, obviously. He kept the weapons cleaned, charged, and ready. He also was our ... cleric, I suppose. He was fluent in almost every human faith, but no one (except maybe War Thug) knew what *he* believed in, if anything. He entered battle only after making sure everybody else was armed and ready, with railguns and rifles and pistols—and, if they needed, spiritual guidance to help them kill every nonhuman being they possibly could. His Enhancement was appropriate to his position as unofficial clergy: He could, just with a touch of his bare hand, spread a sense of unshakeable calm through any human. Not every soldier wanted that, however; and thus Gunner was also able to imbue a sense of righteous fury in the same way. I suppose it was the production and delivery of neurotoxins through his skin that allowed him this ability. Its influence generally ended at the conclusion of a battle, when the human body's normal chemical defenses overwhelmed and nullified whatever it was that Gunner had been able to instill. All of us except Sarge had called upon Gunner for his services during one fight or another.

7. **Fugly:** Infantry. Hands down, she was the most beautiful woman, the most attractive *person*, any of us had ever seen. Smooth skin, piercing green eyes, supermodel face and body. She was transferred to our crew when she put several members of her old platoon to cryo until they could be moved to a quadrant base to get their

missing organs replaced with non-functional dildonics. No court-martial for her; in a sex-integrated Space Navy, there's no room for rape or attempted rape. She kept her helmet on whenever she was around the rest of us for the first couple of weeks, but Sarge gave her that nickname and it brought her out of her shell to see she was with platoon-mates who cared only how she fought. She showed us how: without mercy. It made her even more beautiful in all of our eyes.

And we were not alone. Unlike with the others, I had no idea how her Enhancement worked, even on the conceptual level. She could make anyone or anything that looked at her see only beauty—whatever beauty was to aliens or just bugs, that's what they sensed. She couldn't turn it on or off; it just *was*. The males in the platoon often wondered, when the females weren't nearby, whether they were seeing her as she really was—or, indeed, if there was any "reality" outside of her Enhancement anymore. This may seem obvious, but while she could, and *did*, fight like the soldier she was, her "glamour" ability served us as a powerful distraction to the enemy, whether it was male, female, or whatever the hell some of these bugs were.

8. **Ernie:** Communications. He manned the A/V links between our Heads-Up Display screens as well as kept us in contact with the closest base and, when necessary, even Terra, via subspace frequencies. His Enhancement was that it had all been installed in his head: he mentally routed all of

our feeds as well as communications outside our Gang of Merry Men. We had radio backups, of course, but none worked as well as Ernie's head. He also was in charge of our supply chain, keeping us fed or letting us know when we wouldn't be eating anything but flash-frozen sea biscuits for a while.

9. **Dahlia:** Up-close combat specialist. Her Enhancement was that her bones had been replaced with "memory nanoblocks" and could not be broken. Also, her deep ebony skin and taut muscle were rewoven at the molecular level and, like any reformed fibers, they created a bond almost impossible to penetrate. She could therefore punch and kick and slam and heap a lot of other abuses on an enemy, even without armament. Sarge still had her outfitted with armor and a railgun in battle, but she loved when there were stragglers which she could release some tension on.

10. **Calico:** Assassin. Sarge told me he called her that because of her Enhanced ability to move without making a sound and run completely silently, like a cat, to kill an enemy before it even knew what was happening, even when Calico bore heaps of armor and weaponry. She also seemed preternaturally able to elude scopes, cameras, any kind of detecting equipment whenever there was any kind of shadow (light, radio, and heat, to name a few) to hide her. She also favored keeping pieces of her personal kills as trophies. I don't know if that's something cats do, but it seemed awfully feline to the rest of us. It was especially fitting,

perhaps, that she was also our platoon medic. We always wondered if she kept little pieces of us when she put us back together.

11. **Boswell:** Logistics and reporting. This is me. I fit into the naming scheme, so Sarge kept mine. (He usually called me "Boz.") I had been hoping for a nickname until I realized through several horrifying battles that War Thug respected only bloodlust and survival in his grunts. The nicknames weren't a sign of anything; they were just another tool for him to manage his soldiers and help them kill more effectively. My specialty was being Sarge's right-hand man. I kept track of the where and the what and the when and the rest while War Thug killed and killed. He then had me enter the log entries once he told me if the battle was a success or not. Sometimes what I thought was a victory would end up in Sarge's eyes as a draw or even a defeat. I asked him after one battle in which we killed almost every damn bug on that rock why he was having me log it as anything but a success. His eyes focusing somewhere far away, he said in his grumble, "There's one still alive down there, I just know it." My Enhancement was a blessing and a curse: I had a completely eidetic memory. That meant I possessed perfect recall of anything I saw, heard, or experienced, and could relate them at will at any level of detail I desired. I have never forgotten even one kill in one battle. The "log entries" were kept in my mind until we were finished fighting and the details could be relayed to base.

12. **Ace:** Our pilot. She hated that nickname (but kept it in respect to Sarge) because she thought it made her sound like a daredevil; in fact, she was a meticulous navigator and a master at moving vehicles through both atmospheres and the vacuum of space. Her Enhancement was some kind of biological gyroscope that gave her a perfect sense of direction and spatial orientation: She literally could fly with her eyes closed, and had done so several times in my presence, but this was only when the instruments failed and the need to *move* was most pressing. She refused to "show off," although she was always very polite and told us she appreciated our faith in her. A very good woman, we entrusted our lives to her every time we boarded her ship, the *Blue Celeste*.

13. Finally, there was **War Thug**. He had arms as big as legs and hands as big as a human head, with legs and feet to match. All of us assumed that was his Enhancement—comic-book-huge and strong limbs and extremities with unmatched ripping and kicking abilities—especially since his normal-sized head seemed small in comparison. Small, that is, except when he had his helmet on in battle, in which case you'd better not be looking at him instead of the enemy anyway. This muscle theory was a guess on our part, as Sarge never told us what (if anything) his Enhancement was, and we sure as hell weren't going to ask. His muscles did weave seamlessly into what we knew was a prosthetic right forearm made of indestructible carbon nanotubes, despite its flesh-like covering.

Ace, of course, stayed aboard the ship while the rest of us leaped, and Sarge would clip on and follow us down the space elevator cable after getting the all-clear from me, the last grunt to touch boots on the ground.

About those Enhancements I threw at you: with a mandate from the War Council, the Space Navy required all enlisted soldiers and commissioned officers expected to take part in field operations to undergo an "Enhancement." As you saw, this could be a sharpening of natural sensory or physical abilities, or it could be something entirely new but immensely useful in battle. Those who could not or would not accept Enhancements were labeled as "not fit for duty." They were often tasked with rebuilding Terran cities, which often necessitated clearing out the 10 billion dead who still lay in the ruined streets. I couldn't see why one would rather do that than go Enhanced and fight the many evils lying in wait in this part of the galaxy.

The point is, the War Council would invest whatever it took in terms of money, research, and application of technology— weapons and biotech—to cleanse this sector of the galaxy of any and every threat. And that meant Enhanced soldiers who could kill almost anything.

Anyway, I leaped, and immediately gravity grabbed me from the geosynchronous orbit and pulled me toward Gale at an acceleration of 5 feet per second. This was slower than Earth's attraction but still plenty fast, and I would be fairly close to the ground before I reached terminal velocity, which was my signal to unclip and yank my chute.

Well, that was *usually* the signal. For our leap onto Gale, however, we were forced to open the chute when we were practically touching the ground, since the super-high winds would hurl anyone with an open parachute hundreds of clicks away from the drop zone. Fortunately, we were outfitted with shock-absorbing bounce packs, which meant we didn't have to rely so much on the chutes to keep us from ending up as a red blotch on a hostile planetoid.

Sarge got the automatic signal from my equipment that I was safe on the ground, and then he made his leap. We were too busy stowing gear and reconning the landing area to watch anyone leap, but sometimes we made an exception for Sarge, whose massive bulk fell with impressive grace. He yanked his chute and deployed his bounce pack at precisely the right moment, allowing him to ultimately land dead-center of the drop zone, on his feet. As always.

Even in this goddamn wind. All of us literally had to consciously place each step due to the random pulsation of immensely strong winds, followed by a stillness, followed by the wind again. How long one period or the other would last, we had no idea. But it knocked us over—well, all of us except Hog, Junebug, and Sarge, and even they were rocked a good bit.

The air was mostly transparent but approached a blue tint the farther up you looked. However, I almost instantly learned not to look up, because the bands of Kokytos stretched from horizon to horizon. Since the moon—large when compared even to Terra's moon—was nonetheless tidally locked with Kokytos, and so this was what anyone standing on this part of Gale would see every hour or every day: nothing but the swirls and bands of the gas giant. It felt like the sky was bearing down on us, so close was Gale to its host planet. If Kokytos didn't rotate so fast, a moon the size of Gale would simply have been flung off into space, or never formed. Seeing the horizon only filled with planet was disorienting, even nauseating.

However, we weren't there to sightsee. Not that there was much to see anyway. The vegetation was very low to the ground and grew only in the lee of a rock. I imagined the water supply, if the bugs and plants on this planet even used water, was mostly in underground rivers, where it would not be evaporated by the powerful winds. The ground was mostly exposed rock scoured clean of sand, which one could see collected against the bases of bigger rocks that rose all the way to hill size just within our range of sight.

Sarge made us count off and then brought us in a circle to make sure we all knew our mission on this weird rock. We knew it, of course—this was "pest control," as we grunts called the officially designated "extermination missions." That meant that no resources that Terra was interested in were known to exist here; no alien technology was expected to be retrieved because the low "sentience value" of the aliens (that is, they were "bugs") meant the only thing they created was bug crap; and these bugs were in the size range of a human or bigger, meaning the War Council considered them a possible threat if—and this had never happened, but just in case—a sentient alien species captured them *en masse* and dropped them on cities on Terra.

In other words, we were to kill everything we saw. Officially, the concern was only about the man-sized-or-bigger xenoforms, but it was well understood by all Space Navy infantry platoons that if a life moved, it should be rendered unable to move ever again.

The first few moments on an alien planet were the most tense, because you literally didn't know how a bug species would attack, or if it would attack at all. (We weren't doing a sociology study here; their level of aggression toward *us* was immaterial. We only had to know the level of aggression we needed to have toward *them* before getting down to business.)

Sarge intentionally had us touch down within walking distance of the lip of a valley, since lifeforms tended to collect in these for safety and sometimes because they didn't know how to get out. So we marched ourselves one click or so to what Ace upstairs told us was the rim. All of us had our railguns out, their heavy-hydronium projectiles ready to slice through the air at nearly light speed and end the existence of whatever they hit (humans included, so we had safety protocols drilled into our brains at every training session). The ammo would then be replaced almost instantly by a forced condensation and ionization of the oxygen and hydrogen in the local air. That meant the railgun was always loaded, although this didn't happen on planets without these atmospheric elements or which lacked atmospheres in the first place. That's when Inman had to make sure we brought enough hydronium along to kill anything that moved.

Which happened before we had taken even ten steps. In a depression in the ground nearby, something about the size of a dog stuck its head up out of a hole. Dahlia caught notice of it first—we each had our section of the 360 degrees around us to monitor—and her rifle charged to let off a single shot, disintegrating the mole-thing and earning one credit from each of us for getting the first kill.

"Son of a bitch!" Killshot complained into his helmet mike, and I could hear the rest of us chuckling at him. "I was gonna get the first one this time."

"*Riiight*," Gunner said. "You can't shoot anything unless you're lying on your belly."

Junebug chimed in: "And even then …"

We all hooted at her jibe, even Gunner.

"You lot can pay me when we get back to the ship," Dahlia said in her Irish brogue. "Not a lot of taverns on this rock, are there?"

"You know we're good for it, Dahl," Junebug replied, "but ain't no one paying up until we see if you make it—I'm not wasting a credit!"

"All right, assholes, let's keep it happy," Sarge growled, but we could hear his light tone. We all knew why he had it, too: there was so much *killing* to do.

I should interject this here: I may have made Sarge seem like some kind of magical being who unfailingly and single-handedly protected each member of our platoon from death in every battle. While he has saved us individually and as a group many times, we have also saved him, and we've saved one another. No one, not even Enhanced soldiers, can detect every threat every time. So we keep tabs on everybody else, and we get out alive.

What I'm trying to say, and this is maybe out of line for a log entry, but we love each other. I have no family on Terra, few of us did, but even if we did … the platoon is our family. We celebrate whoever gets a first kill, even of some indigenous rodent analogue. We help out when one of us is trapped, or hurt, or going psycho in battle—and it happens to all of us, even Sarge. Maybe *especially* Sarge. But none of us try to save him when his eyes go wild amidst all the blood or ichor or whatever our enemies have. For one, he's so powerful none of us, or maybe not even all of us together, could really keep him from doing what he wanted to do; and two, that might not be any kind of "psycho" mode for him. It might just be the way he fights best. For the rest of us, though, sometimes we need to get our heads straight so we keep our rifles straight, if you get me.

Killshot put up a fist and we all instantly shut up and froze in place, as much as we could in the buffeting winds, anyway.

"What ya got?" Sarge instantly barked on the comm.

"I got quintrapeds running like hell at us. Two o'clock."

"What's a quintraped? A little … ped? What's a ped?" Hog said in his puzzled drawl.

"Five legs, man," Inman said, not unkindly. "Now be quiet and let me hear how many there are." He opened a sliding hole on the side of his helmet sealed off from the rest of his helmet—he could do this only on planets where there was enough atmospheric pressure not to blow his eardrum—and stood stock-still, listening through the roaring wind to what he could pick up of the bugs.

"How many?" Sarge said.

"Many," Inman said. "Maybe we should get off this patch and make for the rocks." There was a nice, safe-looking crop of boulders about a hundred yards to our left, and another maybe half a click to our right.

"Understood. First one who goes lateral gets in the leg," Sarge said, a sentiment we all knew he would hold, including Inman. But it was our ordnance man's duty to make a suggestion based on his Enhanced hearing. "Dahlia, Hog, Fugly—infantry up front with me. Leonard, Inman, Ernie, Boswell—battle support make a row of three take our flanks, Boz in the middle. Calico, Junebug, Killshot, Inman—battle specialists take the rear. Now, assholes."

We all moved into our familiar positions—we all long knew where we went at the beginning of a pest control operation, but like I've said, Sarge was meticulous and wouldn't let us send the mission FUBAR because against all odds we forgot what to do. We made three rows, the front with four soldiers, the middle with three and the rear with four.

I was in the middle of that second row, surrounded by my platoon-mates, a position I hated every single time, but as the chronicler of our missions, my memory was more valuable to the War Council than my rifle was. That didn't mean I wouldn't be doing plenty of shooting and killing myself once we were in the thick of it and spread out, but for the first wave, I was protected like a pearl inside a very tough clam.

The infantry faced forward so they could take the mass of bugs head-on. Battle support faced the flanks at 90 degrees. And the battle specialists faced the rear, walking backwards as the eleven of us moved but never losing exactly where they were.

"Large mass of bios bearing down on you," Ace told us from his perspective in orbit.

"Roger that," Sarge said, his voice a little tighter. "Get ready, you bums."

An observer would have thought us ready before, but he would see that as being at ease compared to what we did now, which was bending at the knees to stay low and bring our arms and weapons close in to our bodies.

Now Sarge barked, "Killshot, about-face—how tall are the bugs?"

He smoothly rotated 180 degrees and stood to his full height, giving him an unimpeded Enhanced view of the enemy approaching. I could see the change in his eyes as he grokked the size of our enemy. "Man-sized, sir. They'll be within normal sight range in a few seconds."

"Dammit," Sarge grumbled. We knew the problem was one that Terran soldiers always faced: in the heat of battle, everyone was pretty much the same height, and that could lead to shooting your own soldiers.

"But good news, sir: they're running like quads," Killshot added before he turned back and took his battle stance once again. I wonder if everyone else had the quick thought that he meant a *normal* human, not one so (apparently) Enhanced in strength and size as War Thug.

"Great," Sarge said with irony. Again, we knew what the problem was: a bug the height of a human but running on all four (or five) legs had god knew how much weight and momentum. A bull charging you was shorter than a man, but its bulk was carried on four legs and so it shot forward like a missile, long and heavy in a line starting with its ass and ending with your body.

"That could be mostly shell," Ernie said, and we took it to heart since Ernie was far and away the "brain" of our group when it came to speculative analysis (that is, coming up with ideas and observations that might aid us in the fight to come). During the battle itself, Leonard was the brain and could use his electric Enhancement to herd the bugs toward us or into an ambush. "But that's only if they are analogous to Terran insects, of course."

"Let's hope. Rifles up, people!" Sarge barked, meaning he and the other infantry could now see the enemy on its way and we would be in thick of it in the next thirty seconds.

I held my own rifle in front of me, left hand on the stock and right lying on the trigger guard but not curled around the actual trigger. I didn't want to get jostled and blow my own head off or put a hole through one of our own. The other thing I did was closely watch the bugs—I could see them now, and indeed they were the size of a two-man capsule. If a two-man capsule ran on five legs, that is, the extra limb coming out of its head and now extended to cause damage.

Ernie came on the comm and noted they were running on this leg along with the other four by keeping their heads pointed down and bobbing along with their gallop. "That means they possibly can't see when they run, if their eyes are front-facing. Could be useful."

"Roger," Sarge said, barely audible even over the radio link now. His concentration was on what was immediately before him. So was mine: the thunder of ten thousand legs accompanied the horripilating sight of those humpbacked, buffalo-sized aliens coming through the blowing haze 100 yards in front of us.

Which was plenty close enough.

"*GO HOT!*" our commander shouted in the comm, which hurt our ears but got the front line shooting.

A railgun with hydronium bullets made a strange sound in operation. A full magazine of the frozen ammo held no less than *ten thousand* rounds and so the cooling unit contained in the stock hummed continuously (this was one reason why our assassins didn't use them—also, a railgun wasn't really the ideal choice at throat-slitting range). As shells were expended, the rifle made a whooshing sound as it sucked in atmosphere to form hydronium from. This was rarely audible amidst the sounds of battle, but you could feel the thing in operation through the reverberations going through your arm and shoulder.

Also, they made a high-pitched whine which rose in frequency until it was inaudible—to us. Sometimes our enemy could hear higher in the register, which was a blessing and a curse for the good guys, because it would help them locate us as often as it would frighten them away from a fight.

These Gale bugs didn't seem to take notice one way or the other of the sound of eleven high-powered railguns charging up for their first blasts of the day (and one for its second). As they got right in our faces, I could see that they were no dumb "bugs" at all — they barked commands at one another (which we couldn't understand, of course, but it was very clear what the sounds were) — and just as the infantry up front laid down the first shots of hydronium, the crowd of bugs moved to the flanks to surround us. A bunch went down at the hail of railgun fire, but even with our flank soldiers and then our rear contingent blasting away, we were quickly surrounded.

That didn't matter in itself. It just meant we had plenty of targets, all of us. (Except me, still stuck in the center of the formation.) The railguns whined and the sonic booms burst in a constant roar that we had shields over our ears to handle. We hoped the bugs had no such protection and could hear somewhere near our audible range—not knowing the thunderous noise was coming could help throw them off their attack. (The similar atmosphere was a good indicator that this could be the case.)

Ten thousand rounds of solid heavy water multiplied by eleven tore through the bugs like they were tissue paper. Seeing them close-up and dying was the first we took in of what the aliens actually looked like, and they weren't anything approaching humanoid. Their bodies were encased in something more like a turtle's shell than a Terran insects folded wings, but when they reared up to attack—and were promptly sheared into ribbons—I could see their organs in the back through translucent skin. Their faces consisted of a mouth hole and half a dozen eyes, as well as what we could see now wasn't exactly a fifth leg but instead a heavily muscled proboscis that helped them run faster.

The air would have been thick with bug parts, but the wind immediately swept away the fluids and chunks of alien flesh as we fired and fired and fired into the circle of attackers, knocking them back into one another as they fell in the hail of ice bullets, our railguns working overtime to convert atmosphere into hydronium and keep our magazines full. The barely-resistible hurricane winds help the guns reload more quickly, since air was practically shoved into it.

Soon enough, we found ourselves in the center of a circular pile of bug parts, the ooze puddling above the tops of our boots. Sarge put his hand up for us to cease fire and also be silent. We obeyed, of course, and turning our "ears" on again after having shut them down for the deafening noise of all that shooting, we couldn't hear anything except the wind. There was no scuttling, no chittering, no orders in an alien tongue being shouted among our enemies.

"Sir, we couldn't have shot them all. They must have retreated," Inman said. "I can hear maybe a dozen aliens moving around out there."

"Roger," Sarge said, and he looked up and around us, taking in the fact that we couldn't see anything except the nauseating planetary bands above us. "This situation is not ideal."

We could tell that, for sure. God knew how many tons of biomass we had piled around us now, made by ourselves as we blew away every bug coming at us, and then every bug that climbed the pile of dead to come at us, and then the bugs that climbed the new and bigger pile ...

"Junebug, we need to get through this waste dump. Can you push through it?" Sarge asked her because she had the Enhancement of density, which allowed her to build up momentum as she ran and she had burst through a great number of apparently impenetrable barriers.

"We're too packed in here, sir," she said with regret. "I wouldn't be able to build up enough speed to break through much of anything."

"Hog, what can you do to get us out of here?"

The big farm boy with the Enhancement allowing him to vibrate anything into disintegration pushed his hands against the glistening wall of alien entrails and limbs. "I don't know if I can get us all the way through, but I can sure try. Only thing is, everybody's got to get away from the pile so they don't get shook."

We all looked at how close the piled-up body parts were to us, and the whole platoon tightened up like a coward's sphincter. Hog nodded in approval of our safer position and pushed his hands into the black-and-brown goop. It took a few seconds, but his arms' vibrations quickly ramped up from invisible to the point where they blurred exactly where his arms were. (He didn't need to vibrate anything else, which was fortunate because the rest of us would not enjoy the experience of the ground under our feet vibrating in sympathy with his movement.)

In seconds, the arms and legs and eyes and ichor of the dead-bug pile shook, first slowly and then at a frequency to match Hog's. I was thankful we had our helmets on, because when the vibrations took hold, it scattered whatever was in the pile that he didn't reduce to a slurry of noxious, oily sludge. The well we were stuck at the bottom of collapsed and turned to liquid, and we could now see what was on the other side of Bug Part Hill.

What was on the other side were the sentients of Gale. The fifty or so bipeds stood on every boulder and in even spaces around our platoon. They each had a weapon in hand that looked pretty damn deadly, not as powerful as our railguns, maybe, but possibly plasma weapons that would immediately burn us to cinders or "only" forever stop our hearts in our chests.

The bipeds were ten feet fall if they were a centimeter. Each had large, jet-black eyes and wore some kind of speaking apparatus across their mouths like bandanas pulled up on a train robber's face. It didn't take long to learn what these devices were, because English came from the sentient with a uniform of a color different from all the others.

"Place your hands above you, invaders," it said.

"Naw," War Thug said, very slowly moving as if he were putting his hands in the air, "we've come as liberators. We want to liberate your technology from your terrorist pseudopods. Then we are going to kill you all."

The aliens all kind of looked at one another. Their black eyes, if I had to guess, showed a complete lack of understanding.

Of course, I thought, and almost laughed: *We* weren't wearing any translation hardware. They had no idea what War Thug was saying. The translation worked in just one direction.

"Invaders, we request—" the head Xeno said, but almost immediately interrupted himself, "—one of your number is missing." The leaders buzzed back and forth with his lieutenants, who fruitlessly—and aimlessly—looked around for that one of our "number."

"Do your thing, Calico," Sarge said loudly and clearly.

Our assassin, with her Enhanced powers of undetectability and camouflage, popped up behind one of the farthest aliens and broke his neck with his own weapon, then slipped immediately out of sight. He had let out a buzz of distress before falling, something Calico had no doubt intended, because almost every alien soldier turned to see what his yelp was about.

When they were looking back at what Calico did, they weren't looking forward at us. (Of course, the ones facing that direction didn't have to turn, but they did take their attention off of us momentarily, which was much the same thing in a tense combat situation.)

"Leonard, zap these assholes," Sarge ordered, and Junebug and Hog—both hunks of solid muscle—lifted the slim technician above their shoulders, and every sentient trained its plasma rifle on him. Before they could get the order out to fire, Leonard stretched out his slim arms and *made* two of their weapons fire its electric fury, the arcing bolts connected his hands to their weapons, then pushing back and reflecting the plasma back at them, reducing the soldiers to a gray smear.

At that, the leader buzzed something loud, and the remaining soldiers hoisted their weapons to fire on Leonard.

This was a bad, bad tactic, but one that we had used successfully before. Leonard was the one who killed the two soldiers, so the blizzard of deadly plasma was directed toward him—the one SEAL who had an electrical Enhancement. The rest of us, any of whom might have been disintegrated by the beams, were not targeted, and that meant we could open fire.

Which we did. Leonard leaped into the air, catching the plasma arcs and throwing them back at the alien soldiers, who then were practically *erased* by the powerful bolts; and we laid into the remaining sentient alien soldiers, piercing their armor and ending their lives, every single one.

"Ernie, these guys have their operation underground, correct?"

Our radio-telepathy–Enhanced platoon-mate turned his head so he could tune in to whatever electromagnetic frequencies might reveal the location of the Gale aliens' facilities. They were obviously slightly less advanced technologically than we were, but that could be plenty advanced to constitute a threat to Terra. "Right as usual, Sarge. Signals and traces coming from below. I'd say the entrance would be around that rock," Ernie said, pointing to the widest boulder in our immediate vicinity.

"Good job, platoon. Fugly, Dahlia, Hog, Gunner, Ernie—check for an entrance. If you find it, down the rabbit hole you go, Fugly in front to confuse the assholes, Gunner just behind to neutralize aggression. Ernie, route their vidcam signals to our HUDs." Fugly's glamour Enhancement would make her appear as whatever these things thought was beautiful, and that always made them hesitant to fire; Gunner quickly used his Enhancement to calm the soldiers going down enough to focus on, but not so much that they could not react swiftly and with clear heads respond to any threat; and Ernie would use his Enhancement to keep us all updated on our heads-up displays with one another's signals at all times. "Dahlia and Hog, break anything living until it isn't anymore."

"Aye, aye, sir," they said as a group before going to the rock, giving our usual Space Navy acknowledgment of orders.

Sarge didn't have to tell the newly returned Calico, Killshot, Leonard, and me to stay behind, as our skills and Enhancements were needed there on the surface with him. Calico could hide and surprise any ambitious sentient soldiers who thought they got the drop on us. Killshot could get his ass low and pick them off from as far away as the wind and silt would allow him to see. Leonard couldn't go down with the others if there were computers and such, things that might be damaged if he was forced to defend them with his electric talents—the War Council always wanted the technology preserved and the aliens dead—but he *would* help protect us from the plasma guns if any stragglers did show up. And I, of course, stayed with Sarge pretty much at all times. I would monitor all the go-team's vidcams at once on my collapsible monitor, remembering every detail for the logbook and report to be made after the mission.

For that report, my memory and perceptive Enhancements enabled me to weave their different voice and audio signals into one narrative, see what they saw and construct a mental image of their surroundings, and enter this sequence into the log even though I remained above ground.

***

"Stairs leading down," Fugly reported, her vidcam pointed downward to record the image. "I'm always glad when the sentients are bipeds. Much easier to get around in here."

"Yeah, maybe a bit of a fixer-upper, though," Gunner said, moving his head so we could see the dark, dank space with walls seeming to *ooze* black. "I think we could get it for cheap and flip it in today's alien headquarters market."

"I have no idea what you are even talking about," Hog said.

"I do," Sarge said to them through the comm. "Now secure your comments, Mister Funnyman. Plenty of time for jokes when we're all alive later."

The slight nodding in Gunner's vidcam showed he got the message.

Now it was Inman who held up his fist, and we all stopped and were utterly silent as he cocked his head first one way, then the other. "This facility is *huge*. I can hear echoes from ten levels below us."

"All military?" Sarge pinged.

Inman took his time, which was expected and preferred. He had to balance the different volume levels as they resonated below the rock floor, trying to block out the ever-howling wind at the opening to the facility. But he could hear patterns of reverberations, and we could see through his helmet that his face snapped into recognition and he nodded to himself before comming to Sarge, "Negative, sir. It sounds like two levels of military operation and eight or more levels devoted to … I guess a city with residences and lots of hustle and bustle."

"So probably not military targets."

"That's my impression, sir."

"Hmph," Sarge let out, which we all knew meant to give him a minute. After a moment, he said, "Fugly?"

"Here, sir."

"Find the door to that military command level and do your thing. While they're stunned, Hog and Dahlia, assist Inman and Gunner in getting the ordinance placed at the stress points. Copy?"

"Aye, sir, but we'll have to guess at those points inside this rock."

"Understood. Get them in place while Fugly shines, then all y'all get the hell out of there on the double, *capische*?"

"*Sissignore!*" Gunner shot back as we moved to find the opening to their military rooms. (This was the Italian equivalent of "*Sir, yes, sir!*")

"If your ass was any smarter, they never woulda let it join the Navy," Sarge said. "Now let's get to work. We're target-free up here, so let's get in and get out *right now*. GO!"

In the utter darkness, even on their infrared cameras (stone is cold, of course), they could detect a path pressed into the floor through years or decades or more of foot traffic. And it was a damned good thing they had that tactile sensation come up through their boots, because it was the only way they would have been able to find what passed for a door.

It was a hole in the rock. All of us could hear the impossible tongues of our sentient enemy through it, but the question was whether they could drop down the fifteen feet through the hole to the floor of that first subterranean level.

"I got this," Dahlia said with no hesitation in her voice whatsoever. "Sarge, permission to enter the Xenos' headquarters."

"Granted," Sarge commed back immediately. "Take Fugly on your shoulders and get her in front of you as soon as you hit the ground. Let your knees cushion her fall—yours heal, hers won't."

"Aye aye, sir," Dahlia said, and we all shared her confidence she felt in her Enhancement making her practically "unbreakable." She then got on her belly and slid her legs toward and then down into the hole and motioned for Fugly to come front and center. As our glamour girl approached, Dahlia put her arms straight out to support her body hanging from the hole now.

I hoped none of the sentients were paying any attention.

With the other members of the team supporting Fugly as she got balanced on Dahlia's shoulders, the big woman on the bottom counted down to zero and dropped. Fugly dropped with her, and we could all see in our HUDs that it had gone off perfectly, the slim woman rolling off and coming back up with her weapon held inconspicuously behind her back.

And oh, did it go off perfectly. Every huge black eye fixed immediately on her and didn't look away, didn't notice Gunner, then Inman, then the giant farm boy Hog dropping onto Dahlia's shoulders and rolling off just as Fugly did. Through their vidcams, it looked much like a Terran office, although everything was fashioned out of that Stygian, always-wet-looking stone.

Not knowing what "turned on" the aliens, Fugly improvised and assumed touch was a sexual move universally appreciated. She seemed to have chosen the right technique—the sentients didn't take their eyes off of her for an instant. This made it easy for Inman, Dahlia, and Gunner to place the canisters full of flesh-melting toxins unimpeded. The devastating chemicals were devised especially for the Gale atmosphere, which the War Council assumed was what the "Xenos" (as Dahlia and the other infantry preferred to call the sentient aliens) naturally breathed.

Fugly waved a hand as the four SEALs moved to the hole allowing access to the next level. This little move—and I had no idea how any of my fellows' Enhancements actually *worked*, including my own; it was not our place to question why, do or die, etc.—somehow kept her glamour alive for ten seconds or so after she had removed herself from the area entirely, and also kept whomever it was used on from remembering what exactly had just happened other than they had just been in the company of the most beautiful/handsome/other creature they had ever encountered. It had worked on every bug, sentient, whatever Xeno our platoon ever encountered.

So Sarge and the rest of us up top watched Dahlia, Fugly, Inman, Hog, and Gunner repeat the maneuver, and this was the room that would make the War Council back home completely salivate: what I immediately recognized as a huge quantum computer took up one wall, and vidscreens (which looked blank to me, but no doubt were full of information for the sentient military aliens seeing it in their visual spectrum) with the Xenos hunched in front of them. The amount of information the Council could glean from just what this room contained was mind-boggling.

But first, to kill the bastards who dared to threaten Terra. Or who could someday.

Inman, Dahlia, and Gunner placed the deadly gas canisters set to release as soon as our whole away team had gotten out of the stone facility … but there was one more that Inman pulled out of his ordnance sack, and once he had it in his hands, he gently calibrated it.

"What you got there, Inman?" Leonard asked from above, any new technology always catching his undivided attention.

"Secure that until later, soldier," Sarge growled.

"Naw, it's okay," Inman said, now finished messing with the settings on whatever the large canister was. "This hits the floor on the level below, it explodes into a honeycomb of impassable fill-foam. Nothing will be coming up through that lower level. Ever again."

Junebug let out an impressed whistle.

"What about other exits?" Sarge asked.

From the ship up in orbit, Ace piped in, "I've done a full scan of the ten square kilometers around that entrance. Nothing with a heat signature that suggests an alternate exit."

"Roger," Sarge said. "Good work. Now drop that goddamn thing so we can get off this rock and send in the Council whitecoats. I'm sick of this wind and this view of the ass end of Kokytos."

"Aye, sir," Inman answered him, and dropped it down the hole. The explosion wasn't very loud, but we could see the rapidly expanding honeycomb that would prove impenetrable for a thousand years. Even if they grew their own food down there, that would be an awfully long time to survive, especially when the War Council got what it needed and sterilized the entire moon.

Hog essentially threw each one of our party high enough in the air that we could get purchase on the floor above and pull them up. Then Hog jumped and it was just barely possible for the four SEALs to pull him out of the opening. Then they ran like hell, because Fugly's glamour might not keep the two top levels from noticing that canisters of shrieking death had been affixed to their office walls.

We wasted not a second getting back to the space elevator and clipping on. Sarge stayed at the bottom to make sure each of the rest of us was safely attached before stomping on the release pedal that detached us from Gale and send the thick cord retracting back to the *Blue Celeste*. We whipped into the air and the winds gave us little trouble as fast as we were moving vertically. Within four minutes, we were on board again and more glad than you know to get those suits and helmets off.

"Excellent work, people," Sarge said with a real smile. "Tightest goddamn unit in the Navy."

"AYE, SIR!" we all shouted back, and got ready for some R&R—usually a week or two on a Terran-controlled "resort planet," which meant intoxicants and slave whores. *Human* slave whores, selected from the anti-Council resistance of Terra. We treated them like the women and men they were—Sarge would allow no less. So we definitely screwed them within an inch of both of our lives, but we also talked, and shared drinks. When they asked one of their new partners—from one of the continually visiting military platoons—to rescue them from their servitude by stealing them away to another inhabited planet where they could hide—most of the time nobody reported them. (Hell, who *wanted* to be a slave? Especially a female sex slave? We were killers, not assholes.) The large majority of us told the pleading girls that it just wasn't possible, no matter how much we may have wanted to free them.

The War Council was not to be trifled with, and certainly not to be resisted. Every now and then a slave whore would beg us to bring him or her onboard our ship, where they would gladly serve as our ship's "comfort companion." It had never been attempted by the crew of the *Blue Celeste*, because Sarge knew what a distraction it would be. Besides, I had heard from other SEALs and soldiers that any man or woman who *was* allowed to travel with a platoon as a whole received much worse treatment—sexual and psychological horrors resulting from soldiers' PTSD, anger, or loneliness—than any authority would allow at the supervised resort planets.

But our R&R was not to be.

We were barely showered and resting in our Velcro-assed seating attire (keeping us in place in the microgravity) before Ernie stepped up and spoke with Sarge privately; after a few minutes, our communications telepath announced to all of us that we had received an urgent subspace message from Terra: there were scientists missing from a research facility in the L system ("creative name," Killshot said with a smirk) with known hostile aliens, no one knew what kind, but apparently very dangerous because their aggressive abilities were what the War Council scientists were there to study in the first place.

"So an extraction? Or bug hunt? Or what?" Killshot asked, munching on a snack he always seemed to have stowed somewhere on the ship. Only he could find them, and it both amused and frustrated us all, because who doesn't want to steal someone's snacks if he's hiding them from you?

"Pure extraction," Sarge said. "From what Terra says, there's no strategic value on the planet other than getting some DNA—or whatever they have—information so we can weaponize their attack hormones, acid creation, who knows what. But the point is, we drop in, grab the whitecoats, bring them to the ship, and get them to the closest base for return to their operational home."

"Sure hope it's near a resort planet," Calico said with a little smirk.

"Get in and get out in 24 hours, I can *guaran-damn-tee* it," Sarge said.

We were already in a good mood. But Sarge knew us and how to make it even better.

Sarge stamped off in his magnet-boots to the flight cockpit. We could hear him say, "Ace, we got us any easy one for once. In and out. Make for L system, its planet in the Goldilocks Zone, L-22233."

"I hate numbers. I'm just gonna go ahead and rename it 'Bunghole' right now," Calico said,

We all shook our heads and smiled. *Planet Bunghole, here we came.*

***

No planet with complex multicellular life is going to present a mono-climate—desert planets do exist, but they are as barren as Terra's moon. Ice planets are plentiful, but without a breathable atmosphere, nothing was going to develop that the War Council would be interested in. Jungle planets can't exist without a vigorous vapor cycle and temperatures that would be considered at least tropical on Terra and probably even warmer.

Kokytos had probably had a varied ecosystem at one point, but the harsh winds and vicious wind-loving surface bugs drove the sentients underground even as they scoured the surface of the planet. It made them easy to kill, and it would be trivial for the Council's Technology Agents to take every bit of technology since the aliens were considerate enough to keep it on the first two levels, those that hadn't needed to be honeycombed.

Planet Bunghole—excuse me, *L-22233*—looked to have vast rainforests and was just on the hot side of what Sarge had referred to as the "Goldilocks Zone," that sweet spot just far enough from the host star to support oxygen-breathing, carbon-based life that might have life evolved far enough to become sentient and thus possibly to plot against Terra.

The bug hunts—there was exactly *one* artificial structure Ace detected on the planet, and this had to be the whitecoats' facility, so any life would probably be bugs—made excellent training for SEAL platoons, and we had wiped out many a population of harmless aliens. Don't get sentimental—the bugs on Bunghole were probably just big versions of what you wouldn't even hesitate to crush under your boot back on Terra. We could spend weeks on a planet with this level of life, because every bug had its enemy, whether poisonous plants or, most often, other bugs that we could kill as well. With me there, our platoon got every tactic recorded that the Xenos used against one another and usually against us, too. There were also military applications for some of the more aggressive plant species as well, so it wasn't *just* a training exercise. They were fun as hell, though, and Sarge was as jazzed as the rest of us after he pronounced a planet "clean."

Unless some other pressing mission was transmitted to us, we stayed on a bug planet until everything was dead, trying out new projectile weapons like the rail guns, chemical weapons, grenades, everything. We could neutron whole areas deemed too full of bugs to fight conventionally, but that was less fun and so we avoided it when we could. And we'd never waste a Super-Nuke on a population of bugs, no matter how frustrating it might have been to hunt them all down and kill them.

We were allowed—*encouraged*, actually—to use our Enhancements as much as possible, and we often learned new techniques when "fighting" things that couldn't really fight back unless they got right on top of us. And when they did occasionally get to us, one flash of electricity or dose of heavy vibration always did the trick. Good fun, and useful, too.

All of this is to say that Bunghole looked like a diversely populated planet with a fully symbiotic relationship between its different ecosystems. This was exactly the kind of environment where the "bugs" were more like one step below *homo erectus*, just barely sentient, able to use strategy and sometimes tools in order to hunt food or fight "sticks and stones" against rival tribes. Not only that, there were plenty of different predators that may have been bugs to *us*, but a constant and deadly threat to the *homo erectus*-level Xenos. We could be mistaken for the near-sentient race, especially since we wouldn't need our helmets and pressure suits on the impressively Terra-like surface. I had no doubt our Enhanced crew would be able to deal with any aggressive fauna we encountered.

Ace got us into orbit and called over the comm, "The target is directly below us. I'll deploy the cable as close to it as I can get without you assholes planting it right in the middle of their research building."

That made us smile, and Gunner stood for his part of briefing us: weapons. "As Sarge said, this is an in-and-out extraction. We want to avoid anything that will slow us down in getting the three whitecoats out of there, so no harassing bugs or the tool-users. We aren't even charged with bringing back their research files. The air has a good oxygen/nitrogen mix, which will allow us to move fast. All of this means light weaponry. No railguns, just sidearms and—of course—our Enhancements."

"No bullshit on this one, men," Sarge said, and I knew everyone took his and Gunner's words as official mission parameters.

"SIR, NO, SIR!" we shouted as one.

"Good," Sarge said, and called forward to our pilot: "Ace, let's get us bunch of mooks dropped so we can rescue these Dorks in Distress."

***

We dropped without incident, and Ace was right on target: the space elevator was secured not more than 50 yards from a small structure that looked like a gazebo with glass panels etched with the War Council's insignia. We knew we had the right place once we saw that, of course, but this looked like a gazebo you'd see in a vid of some early 20th-century town square. Still, it was a great shot by Ace: our base of operations would be literally at the base of the space elevator.

Our group went back-to-back in a tight circle, keeping our charged sidearms at the ready, pointed 360 degrees to put down any attack from whatever these unfriendlies were. Nothing stirred in the jungle as far as I could see or hear. But that's why we had our comrades in arms.

Almost reading my mind, Sarge said very low into his comm, "Killshot, what you got? Any hostiles?" As we had done before when Killshot's Enhancement was specifically needed, we turned around in our circle so that our sniper could take in everything.

"Just jungle stuff as far I can tell. Some avians flitting between branches, mammalogues snuffling around, nothing organized or bigger than a wild pig. But you guys hear this, right?"

"Hear what?" I said, needing the information for my log report. "I don't hear anything—not even an avian calling out."

Killshot said, "That's what I mean. Whispering into our comms over here, we're the loudest things *in a goddamn jungle.*"

"Secure that language over comm lines, soldier," Sarge ordered quietly.

"Aye, sir."

"Inman, report—are us non-Enhanced just not hearing, or is there nothing to hear?"

We didn't have to shuffle in a circle for Inman to put his hearing to the test; all we had to do was stay still and breathe shallowly or not at all during the time it took our ordnance specialist to complete his aural sweep. Which wasn't long this time. "Killshot's report seems correct, sir. I can hear animal sounds, but nothing organized or aggressive. And those animal sounds are *very* low. Permission to speculate, sir."

"Go."

"My immediate guess is that whatever the predators are that are terrorizing our whitecoats are very sensitive to sound, and use that sense to capture prey. The animals of this rock may have evolved extreme quietude as a defensive response to these sharp-eared predators."

Leonard piped in: "That same silence from the animals may have led to the scientists being heard easily by these apparent predators. They wouldn't have known to stay silent until it was too late."

Until it was too late remained in my mind like an echo, even as an afterimage in my visual cortex. It was an experience I had long become used to during my Enhanced period, my memory storing everything in more ways than I could ever have been registered consciously.

"Where are our desperate whitecoats, anyway?" Sarge muttered. "Ernie, are you getting any signals? Anything electromagnetic going on, some sign of life?"

"Aye, sir, I'm picking up an intense group of electro-signs coming from beneath that gazebo."

The comm registered a couple of groans at the idea of going subterranean again so soon.

"Signs, or signals?"

"I can't detect any *signals* as such, if we mean something intentionally sent out in order to be received. Well, there is one signal, but it's the automatically repeating one from the scientists themselves on the military subspace wavelengths, the one that the Council picked up. Here."

At this he routed the message that had been responsible for bringing us to L-22233—that is, Planet Bunghole. (I will leave off the official designation, as every member of the platoon referred to it exclusively by its nickname for the rest of the mission.) It was a woman's voice:

> This is Doctor Elena Ripple, Captain in the War Council Science Division and the leader of Operation PROMOTE, the official designation of our three-person study of this planet's fascinating predators. With me are my two colleagues, Lieutenant and Doctor Andy Bishop and Second Lieutenant Michael Gorelman, leaders in the Council fields of strategic xenobiology and genetic weaponry, respectively. Our mission on L-22233 is critical to Earth's permanent War on Alien Predation—we have found specimens here that have no analogues on any planets in any systems the War Council has investigated. We have amassed data too sensitive to be sent on subspace channels; it must remain secure until a Council vessel comes to our aid.
>
> I say "our aid" because we have come under attack by the very predators we have been studying. There seems to be a real sentience about them when it comes to aggression—they plot and execute complex schemes to capture prey—but are entirely animal-like on any other measure of intelligence. These are exactly the kinds of ground troops the Council needs in order to continue its sterilization of xenoterrorist threats in this quadrant of the galactic arm.
>
> We need immediate rescue by any Space Navy SEAL team—in other words, the most effective fighters the War Council has available. If the predators break through our

defenses, we are doomed and our data will likely be destroyed in the rampage.

Please send help. Our time on L-22233 is short.

[A five-second pause.]
This is Doctor Elena Ripple, Captain in the War Council Science Division …

"Then it repeats. And that's it, as far as broadcast signals are concerned," Ernie said as he uncoupled the transmission from his electromagnetic-wave Enhancement, surely one of the most impressive the Council had yet devised. He used that talent now to transmit onto our HUDs official digiphotos of the three scientists, then continued, "But there's signs of a *lot* more activity going on down there. Computers, genetic lab equipment, lots of radiation that's just noise, speaking electromagnetically."

"So they're still alive?" Sarge asked, no doubt ready to adjust the parameters of his mission if need be.

"Can't tell for sure, sir, but there is enough variation in the low-level radiation from equipment and such to suggest that there is someone down there still using it."

Sarge chewed on this for a few seconds. "Beneath the gazebo."

"Aye, sir."

"Could be the predators, sir," Hog said. "Maybe they got in and …" He stopped, having stumped himself.

"Good input, Hog," Sarge said, "but I don't think these are sentients, using the computers and such after eating our whitecoats."

"Oh, yeah. I mean, right, sir."

Sarge chuckled at that and said to Hog, "Put on your shoulder vidcam and check out that gazebo, see what the hell it's doing here. Look for doors leading down."

"Sir, we didn't bring shoulder vidcams," I said. "We also didn't need our helmets in this atmosphere, so we don't have our helmet vidcams, either."

"In-and-out mission, my ass," Sarge said, not to me or even to himself. We knew exactly who he was talking to.

"Aye, sir," Hog said, and moved slowly toward the gazebo. He sidled toward the structure, pistol drawn, keeping his eyes peeled for sudden movements.

None came. He made it to the structure and said, "This *is* a gazebo, for real, sir. Everything's made out of wood except the glass windows. There's a square in the floor like a trapdoor, no handles or nothing."

"That must be how the whitecoats get in and out," Leonard said.

"Yeah, I guess, but I don't see how they could open this door thing from the outside."

"It must be to keep the predators out. Maybe the bugs *are* a little bit sentient," Leonard said to Sarge, then continued: "Hey, Hog, does it look like there's any mechanism on the wall or something, some kind of bio-reader? Maybe that way they have it set up so only the whitecoats can get in."

"Checking, scanning the walls with the grid technique," Hog said. "Nope, nothing but a simple six-sided, old-school Terran-style gazebo."

"Good work, Hog," Sarge said. "Come on out and rejoin us."

"I know this may be a dumb question, Sarge, but why would the scientists—or the War Council, if they sent it to be installed here—build a *gazebo*?" Calico asked. "I mean, if they just wanted to mark where their underground labs were, they could've just planted a flag or something."

Gunner said, "I think it's kind of soothing, like photos of old-timey Terra. Gazebos in parks and whatnot. It gives me a sense of peace."

"Won't know until we get in there, Padre," Sarge said. "Hog, you comin' back to us or what?"

"No, Gunner's right, sir," Hog said, and his usually stolid farmboy voice had ... softened somehow. "It's really peaceful in here. The longer I'm in here, the more relaxed—"

"Hog, retreat to us immediately!" Sarge shouted so loud that we didn't need our comms to hear him, and Hog probably didn't either. None of us reminded our leader that he had called for silence; what he did was, by definition, the right thing to do for our mission.

Hog stayed where he was, and questioning an order—let alone ignoring one—was something none of us had ever seen him do. "Sir, I was just thinking maybe if a person just stood on the square, it would recognize it was a human and open. I'm gonna try—" Hog's voice cut out as we all saw him drop out of sight. His comm voice signal vanished. It didn't just go to static—it disappeared entirely. Ernie had lost the signal, a first for our radioman.

"Hog! Report! *Hog!*" Sarge bellowed into his comm, not concerned now about attracting predatory attention. "Son of a bitch! Junebug, get over there and check that door. *Do not* stand on it, soldier, you get that?"

"Aye, sir!" our stolidly build infantryman shouted as she ran for the gazebo, her weapon out and ready. She slowed at the entrance to the structure, however. "I don't—there isn't—*Sarge!* The trapdoor square is closed again ... wow, it really is quiet in here ... peaceful ... um, sir, should I try to —"

"*No*, soldier, thank you. Double-time it back here to us. *Now*." He looked at Ernie. "You still linked with his comm? I'm not hearing jack squat."

Ernie's eyes seemed to move about their sockets at random; he was scanning his telepathic electronic transmissions, looking for some sign of Hog. "No link, sir ... nothing. His comm is either broken or shut off—there can't be shielding in the floor of the structure, because I'm seeing huge electronic spikes down there."

"The scientists?"

"It's not voices being transmitted, or anything else—just the radio frequency of equipment, whatever it is, going into overdrive."

"It could be a defense mechanism zapping Hog and knocking out his comm," Inman said. "A booby trap type of situation."

As Junebug joined us again, Leonard stepped forward. "I need to go down there, Sarge. I can handle the blasts."

"Secure that for a second, son," Sarge said. "We don't need to lose track of two soldiers."

Leonard opened his mouth to say something but closed it just as fast. My bet was that he was going to say *You won't lose track of me*, but Sarge didn't care for braggadocio when it wasn't called for by conditions in the field. Leonard had no idea what was down there; electrical weapons that Leonard could manipulate might have been just one defense … if whatever just stole Hog was even intended as defense.

"Could there be hostiles down there?" Dahlia asked. "We should've brought the railguns."

"Negative. This is an extraction assignment. The Council doesn't want the Xenos killed."

We all stood there, dumfounded. We had *never* heard the War Council tell us not to kill the indigenous population—or at least capture and torture them for information, if we could translate their brainwaves into intelligible communication. For the War Council—and thus for us—every dead alien, whether a bug, a sentient, or a cyborg, was one less future terrorist threat to Terra. So this was a bizarre and unprecedented rider to our mission parameters.

Especially with *War Thug* leading us—his entire being was focused on reducing enemy targets to inert lumps of biomass. Were we to think our commander was going to hold his fire? Or not break important things like heads off the necks and stalks of bugs, let alone potential terrorist sentients? I literally could not think of anything to say, and I could see in the faces of my comrades that they were in the same state.

"I know, I know," Sarge said, hands up to fend off our confused looks. "Luckily, it doesn't look like we have any hostiles in operation to worry about making us disregard our orders. We got nothing to keep us from getting to the whitecoats—and Hog. So let's—"

"Sarge," Inman interrupted. He had his head cocked, listening to something the rest of us couldn't hear. "At least a dozen bipeds headed this way from the northeast, double-time."

"Aw, goddamnit." He didn't ask Inman what he was hearing because that would interfere with our ordnance man's further detection. Also, he didn't need to ask. "Troops, defense position, move toward the gazebo. GO!"

We snapped into our outward-facing circle formation, moving as one toward the odd glass-and-wood structure. As we approached, all of our pistols were unsheathed and ready to fire, but the problem with sidearms, even those that shot quantum packets of plasma at the speed of light, is that their effective range is quite limited compared to a rifle, just like with old-fashioned metal-projectile pistols and rifles. The approaching bipeds, whether they were hostiles or (very unlikely) friendly and curious, would be upon us before we would have much of a chance to get a shot off.

"They're coming through that break in the trees," Inman told us, and we automatically broke our defensive circle and made a line so we could all face the Xenos as one. "They're not slowing down, either. Sir, I don't think engaging is a workable strategy if we're forbidden to exterminate the aliens."

"I'm open to suggestions, soldier."

Inman had nothing, keeping his weapon pointed down at a 45-degree angle but ready to level and fire in an instant. "Understood, sir."

We could all hear the heavy tramping of feet now, and I tensed along with everyone else—I wasn't in the middle of a protected circle now, no matter how important to our missions my logging memory was. And I was glad; I'd much rather be holding up my end and killing along with the rest of the platoon instead of being shielded like a child.

Only we weren't supposed to be killing on this assignment. Surely we would be justified in putting down immediate aggressors, wouldn't we? I knew that I would do what Sarge said to do, just as everyone else in our group would, and he would take the heat from the War Council if they didn't like it.

In full stride, jumping over obstacles like frightened gazelles, the bipeds were suddenly in view and heading right at us. They were strange-looking aliens, and I had seen a lot of strange creatures in my time in the Space Navy. They had very big and muscular legs, which allowed them to run from the jungle 100 meters away with such incredible speed. Their arms were sinewy with muscle, not as big as their legs but looking plenty strong. Each was seven feet tall if they were an inch.

Their skin was as yellow as candle wax, their eyes utterly black. Other than that, their faces were very close to human. Right then, if one could read their expressions as human-like as well, they were in abject terror.

Right at us they came, and we raised our sidearms, ready to unleash a fury of plasma bolts if we had to—and only if Sarge gave the order to fire. Otherwise, we were to remain in position and not do a damned thing. This must sound insane to someone who has never been a Space Navy SEAL, but our responsive body needed an executive head, and that was Sarge.

Our effective range with the pistols was about 15 yards, a distance which the bipeds were closing rapidly. The way they ran, the way they carried themselves, the aliens looked like nothing so much as nano-steroid–pumped humans. Not that this mattered; most of the sentients we encountered (such as those on Gale in our earlier mission) were bipedal like humans and often had faces, which, if not human-like, at least shared the apparently highly adaptive eyes-nasal openings, and mouths as most complex lifeforms on Terra. So some sympathy with these aggressors wouldn't stop us from lighting them up the instant we were told to. But hell, they even wore very spare garments that looked like workout gear—sleeveless unitards with openings big enough to accommodate those massive thighs—all the same color, a kind of sickly yellow that blended in with their odd pale skin. Those had to be some kind of uniform, especially since they all sported an identical insignia. (My Enhancement allowed me to recall in exact detail what the glimpsed insignia was, but it was nothing I recognized or anyone else could place either once I drew it out for them.) Truly, the bipeds looked like slightly malformed humans carved from waxy tallow. Regardless, they were within 50 yards now and still coming right at us. There was no way they couldn't see our party, so we had to assume they planned to engage us.

"On my mark, shoot them in the lower legs. Ankles or feet best," Sarge spoke calmly into his comm. "Do *not* shoot to kill, or you'll be next. On my mark … wait for my command ..."

Fingers tightened on weapons. Triggers were rested upon, ready to be squeezed.

But just as they reached the far limit of our plasma guns, the dozen or so bipeds split and ran like a river around us, just out of reach of our weapons. As in any group, some ran faster than others, and two of the Xenos lagged behind the others. I noticed that they had bloody wounds on their muscular legs. They looked to cut deep through muscle and sinew, and the uniformed aliens' running was noticeably slowed (although still faster than a non-Enhanced human could go).

The faster runners kept at right about a 30-meter radius from us as they came back together between us and the gazebo. The ten of them immediately crammed themselves into the structure, and indeed there was room for a few more—like the two laggards who were just making their way around our firing radius now.

Then everyone froze as an air-rending *roar* reached us from the jungle. We didn't need Inman to tell us that it was coming from the same path the waxen bipeds had come out of a minute before. Our ordnance man and Enhanced-hearing soldier let out a pained yelp of surprise and covered his ears. If it was loud to the rest of us, my god, that had to hurt like hell.

The trees shook. Before we could even register what that portended, a ten-foot-tall *thing* that I had no words to describe burst through the opening and roared again. Very quickly, I took in and filed its characteristics: dark gray skin wrapped around massive arms that made War Thug's look like twigs; legs like those of the smaller bipeds but even more astonishingly developed; that same human-like face as the other Xenos, but this one with a snarl that made me immediately think of a boar with tusks pointing up out of its unmistakable underbite.

"Goddamn," Fugly muttered, and she almost never spoke during an operation.

Its soot-gray skin and black hair (on top of its head, unlike the bald smaller bipeds) made it look to any of us with a religious upbringing like a demon straight from Hell, the tusks only adding to the terrifying visage. All of this information coming to us and reaction from us lasted less than two seconds, and in that time the enormous alien spotted the two waxy Xenos trying desperately to join their mates inside the gazebo—and hurled itself at them.

"Hold fire," Sarge said, very softly. "And stay completely still. It doesn't seem to notice us."

Which was good for us, but bad indeed for the two stragglers. The ten-foot monster—which was wearing a much bigger version of that unitard uniform, jet black and with the same insignia as the smaller bipeds wore on theirs—was upon both of the seven-foot aliens in an instant, taking one head in each hand and yanking them off like they were caps on a ballpoint pen. It let the bodies drop and carefully placed each head in a cloth bag it had kept inside the unitard shorts.

Inman spoke first: "What in the f—?"

"Secure that talk *now*," Sarge growled, and the comms were all once again silent as we watched the ten-foot alien move toward the gazebo, causing the seven-foot bipeds inside to babble in fright. But when it got within about ten meters of the structure, the monster stopped as if he were a vampire and Van Helsing had just pulled out a crucifix. It reared back a few paces, took in a massive lungful of air, and roared at the gazebo's occupants so loudly that all I could think of was the wolf trying to blow down one of the first two pigs' houses.

The gazebo held. The yellow bipeds held their ground. The monster with its bag of heads stomped off toward the opening in the trees, but keeping to that same radius away from us and our short-range weapons. It really didn't seem to notice us … at least until it got to the trees.

Then it turned to look right at us. We were too well trained—and most of us too frightened, truth be told—to react. The monster then ruefully shook its head and disappeared into the forest. What that might have meant—if, indeed, it meant anything in an alien species—would be for the Council debriefers to decide once I unloaded my log report. To me, it looked all too human, and that freaked me out more than its size or its effortless murder of two very big and powerful-looking Xenos.

Our attention riveted to the enormous killer alien, none of us had been paying attention to the gazebo behind us. By the time Killshot turned to get an Enhanced look at the bipeds, there was only one remaining.

"Sarge!" he yelled, and the rest of us all turned just in time to see the last biped disappear, dropping out of sight. "They're jumping through the trapdoor!"

"Platoon, make for the gazebo. *Run.*"

At Sarge's order, we didn't worry about formation and just sprinted all out for the structure, Sarge starting last and getting there first thanks to his Enhanced leg muscles. This was usually how it went, and everyone was fine with it. When our platoon ran, it wasn't in competition for a blue ribbon—it was a full-on emergency, not a race.

Sarge was tall, but he wasn't seven feet tall, and so he whipped into the gazebo just in time to see the trapdoor slide shut. By the time Sarge started unleashing his usual fiery string of expletives, everyone was inside the structure and seeing for themselves that the bipeds had all gone underground, whether by force or by invitation, no one knew.

Something was off, though, and it took a few seconds to realize what it was. The grunts picked up on it one by one, looking with concern at Sarge and then at one another.

It was this: War Thug, a genocidal killer, a man capable of directing his anger like a spotlight to destroy that which he was told needed destroying, a man who was the very face of Terra's War Against Alien Aggression, wasn't unleashing his fury at being frustrated in this current mission objective of getting at the scientists who were at that very moment probably being attacked (if they weren't already dead from earlier attacks). The mission was at least temporarily FUBAR, but he didn't rise to anger. He didn't pound his ham-like fists against the trapdoor to break it apart and get downstairs. He didn't even yell, at us or the aliens or the War Council with their *no-killing* extraction mission. He was quiet.

In fact, War Thug was *smiling*.

"Sarge?" Junebug said, stepping forward. "You okay, sir?"

"This place *is* peaceful," he said dreamily, as if he had been hit with a tranq gun. "It's no place for killing. That's why that giant son of a whore didn't want to get close, even if it cost it some more heads for its bag. This is a safe little place, isn't it, assholes?"

"Aye, sir," we called back, but not in any kind of simultaneity, smiling at Sarge's mix of calm observation and profanity. We were each getting the hippie vibe, similar to a resort planet's calming ganja, but without the giggles or the passing out. I was worried the relaxation would somehow interfere with my Enhancement, but after I tested myself a few times on playing back in my head the exact words and timing my mates had used, I saw that it was unaffected. So I gave in and enjoyed this peaceful feeling, the most intense I had experienced since childhood, the time before I was old enough to be fully informed about the constant danger facing the human race. (I had known there was a huge war and three-fourths of the world had died, but that was comfortably in the distant past for a six year old.) The anxiety never truly left me after that, although when our platoon was in the middle of a firefight, it was for the moment blissfully forgotten.

Sarge nodded to the north, where the blue oval of the system's sun was setting, Planet Bunghole revolving at 90 degrees to its L-star. "The night terminator is almost here. We bivouac inside here tonight. Boswell, how long is night on this rock?"

"A little less than seven Terran hours, sir." I had spent the trip over here studying up on Bunghole, so it would remain in my memory forever.

"Hell, we'd better get to it then. Looks like there's enough room on the floor and the benches for everyone. Junebug and Dahlia, your awesome dense selves get the floor; can't have the benches collapsing, and I say that for myself, too. Inman, I want you just outside the gazebo so you can hear any Xenos coming around—you got your camp mattress?"

"Aye, sir," Inman said, and held up the sponge-sized bivouac kit we all had, which expanded to full size at the prescribed series of touches on its exterior.

"Good man. All right, assholes, enjoy this high—tomorrow we're getting those whitecoats."

***

Inman woke us with a whisper in our comm earpieces, using direct transmission instead of Ernie's radio switchboard Enhancement: "Platoon, we are surrounded by hostiles, but they aren't moving past the gazebo's perimeter. I advise *very* slow movement as you assess the situation."

"Understood," came Sarge's almost-immediate whispered reply. He could fall asleep faster at lights-out and awaken whenever necessary faster than a cat. In one word, the rest of the platoon knew he was wide awake and ready.

I opened my eyes slowly, taking longer than our leader to awaken fully. I could see that my mates also had opened their eyes but not moved, trying to see what they could from their frozen spot in the gazebo.

The ten-foot monsters illuminated by the large moon dominating the Bunghole sky were, as Inman had said, gathered in a circle around our safe place. They all looked similar, with their gray skin, black unitard things, and truly massive arms and legs.

But there was enough variance in their exact heights and facial features to tell that they were not clones. (I had heard about the War Council working to make fighting clones, but it was apparently far cheaper just to send easily and cheaply replaced soldiers. Cloning was a damned expensive and complex process, and it was unlikely that these brutish Xenos possessed the kind of technology or even the conceptual sophistication to create clones of any kind, let alone adult clones.)

"Troops other than Inman, move from supine to sitting position, as slowly as your stomach muscles will allow. Inman, hold your position."

We all did what Sarge instructed. The monsters definitely noticed, their human-like eyes attracted even by our glacial movement. But they didn't seem to care—they just stood in their circle around us and stared. They weren't acting in a hostile manner, but that meant nothing—they might have just been waiting for us to come away from the gazebo, where they could rip *our* heads off. God knows we couldn't run as fast as even the yellow stragglers they had killed yesterday.

"Leonard, report."

"I can feel a ton of electrical energy under this structure, sir, but the gazebo is well insulated. I wouldn't be able to channel enough voltage without breaking down our sidearms, sir."

"Understood. Killshot, report."

"I don't know if the plasma from our weapons would do much damage to these creatures. Their skin looks rhinoceros-tough. It might sting them a bit, but I'm with Leonard—it would take all of our weapons together to make a single bolt strong enough to wound just one of them." He paused, and we could hear him counting under his breath. "There's six of them. That would leave five pissed-off Xenos, sir."

"Roger that," Sarge said, still just above a whisper. "Junebug, report."

"I could charge them, sir, but I think they outweigh me by a couple of tons. The best I could do is serve as a distraction."

"Understood. Fugly, report—can you glamour these things enough to let us all get away?"

Silence on the comm.

"Fugly, report."

Everyone slowly craned their necks to head-count everyone inside the gazebo. Fugly had been on the floor … right next to the trapdoor … and now she was gone.

"Fugly—goddamnit, *Lieutenant Crawford, report!*"

Nothing. We could hear as Ernie tried to raise Fugly, going through the entire spectrum of comm channels used by the Space Navy. Fugly didn't respond on any of them.

"Boswell, you're supposed to be the smart one here—what in hell happened to our infantryman? How could she just disappear?"

I usually enjoyed the fact that my perfect memory made me look much smarter than I actually am, but not now. All I could tell Sarge was what I remembered. "She was positioned near what we're calling 'the trapdoor,' not on top of it but next to it. I think maybe she was next to the part of the door that opens and was dragged in and down before she could make a sound. She might have been tranqed or killed before whatever is down there took her inside, sir."

"That could be why she didn't glamour them, sir. Or if she did, maybe it made them want to bring her down even more," Leonard said.

"Dahlia, report. What do you think this has to do with our giant peeping toms?"

Dahlia was an excellent infantryman even without counting her Enhancement of practical unbreakability, so she was the most trusted to assess potential on-the-ground fighting situations. "They're not breathing hard. They shift on their feet like a nervous kid. And I don't know if anyone else noticed this, but their features seem very human-like."

"I sure as hell noticed that," Gunner interjected.

"Can it, soldier. We all noticed, Dahlia. Continue."

"So if I was to base their battle intentions on *human* facial expressions, sir, I'd say they were more curious or even anxious about our presence here than aggressive."

Once she said that, I took a harder look at their feet and faces. I couldn't disagree with her observations.

We waited for Sarge to chew this over, always watching the monsters for any sign of attack. I noticed everyone, including myself, had their pistols out and charged. A plasma bolt might not even knock them down, but the sidearms were all we had.

"Inman," our leader said at last.

"Sir."

"How do you feel about standing up out there? Very slowly and non-threateningly."

"Can do, sir."

"Make sure you holster your pistol before you get up. Just friendly ol' Inman."

We could hear the smile in his voice as he said, "Roger that, Sarge."

Just outside the gazebo, Inman very slowly moved into a sitting position. The 10-footers gave him their full attention, still looking more curious than warlike. I had no idea why that should be the case, as we saw the day before that these monsters were violent sons of bitches indeed.

Using the side of the gazebo to let him slide up into standing, Inman kept his hands where the Xenos could see them, showing he posed no immediate threat. Who knew if that was something that would even register with the monsters, but it seemed like the smart move to me.

Inman whispered into his comm, "Standing, sir." He didn't have to add *Now what?*

The corners of the Xenos' mouths turned upward, and the ones that had been behind us when we were being surrounded now came to the front to see what was going on. When they saw that Inman was standing and smiling at them, all of the creatures *smiled back.*

Was this mimicking behavior? We had seen that several times in our travels throughout the quadrant, but this seemed different. The "smile" reached their eyes as well, making them look like imbecilic-but-happy murderous giant aliens.

"That's interesting," Calico said as softly as a cat's purr.

"Calico," Sarge said, his voice conspiratorial through the comm, "can you do your thing inside this gazebo? Make yourself invisible in the shadows and angles and whatnot?"

"Aye, sir."

"Good man. Before you vanish, I want you to walk as briskly as you can on the railings. Jump, if you have to, over the breaks. Make some sound. Get their attention. Then go ninja."

"You got it, Sarge," Calico said, and leapt onto the gazebo's railing closest to our visitors and shouted playfully, "Catch me if you can!"

The Xenos immediately shifted their attention to our assassin with expressions of surprise—but not anger. They even seemed to enjoy watching her rapid circling of the structure, at the end of which her body passed into a shadow thrown by the blue sun and seemed to completely disappear. The aliens looked truly confused, but then they broke into wider "smiles" and motioned to Inman with their tire-sized hands. It was as friendly as gesture as we had ever seen from a Xeno (not surprising, since we usually shot and killed them on sight). It looked like nothing less than an invitation to come closer.

Inman spoke calmly. "Sarge? Instructions, sir?"

"I'm gonna have Calico do her thing again, and when they take their eyes off of you, launch your ass back into the gazebo. Even if they refuse to get any nearer, they got those long goddamn arms they could grab you with and twist off your head."

"Understood, sir."

"All right. Calico, start with the leftmost—"

Sarge was cut off by Inman's scream, which made the entire platoon jump to our feet. Exactly as our commander had just described, the nearest 10-footer, the one whose smile and friendly gesture just a moment before had seemed so *human*—just reached out with its long arms and giant hands and scooped up our ordnance man. It all happened so quickly that none of us could lift our pistols to fire even our probably-inadequate plasma bolts.

As soon as the head Xeno grabbed Inman, the six of them ran for the forest, holding our mate above their heads like he was crowd surfing at a "KILL THEM ALL!" government youth rally. They looked like nothing more than cavemen returning home after a successful hunt.

I scanned the faces of my fellow SEALs and saw the same shocked expression that I could feel on my own face. Everybody except Sarge. His jugular pulsed, his face was red, his teeth were bared, and his eyes remained fixed on where the Xenos had slipped back into the jungle.

"This structure is not secure. It's not a peaceful place," Sarge said. "It's a trap, honey-coated with happy gas. The goddamn Xenos read us like a book."

"They have human faces," Dahlia said. "Maybe they have human intelligence, too."

Fire in his eyes, Sarge turned to face Dahlia and punched her, hard, in the face. She staggered back and fell onto one of the gazebo's benches, blood spurting from her ruined nose, but within seconds her body rejected the injury and she looked just as she had before speaking except for the blood staining the front of her uniform.

"Don't you call these bastards *human* again, soldier. Or I'll find a way to keep you broken." He turned back to surveying the jungle line, anger now so thoroughly saturating his being that he literally shook with fury. No one spoke for the next thirty-five minutes; we just kept our asses where they were and waited. His color *very* gradually returned to normal, the veins in his neck and arms ceased hammering, and he turned again to Dahlia. "That was wrong of me, soldier. If you want to file a formal complaint, get with Ernie to send it out. If you don't want to, you can punch me in the face as hard as you want—and I don't have Enhanced healing ability. All right, Dahlia. I am sorry."

"Forgotten already, Sarge," she said with a smile, waving it off. "But I'd like to reserve the right to that punch for a rainy day."

"Granted, asshole." War Thug smirked at her, then cracked his neck with a series of *pops* that made even us hardened SEALs cringe. "Platoon, get your crap stowed. We're gonna get those whitecoats and our men out of there *right now*."

"AYE AYE, SIR!"

***

Junebug's Enhancement was her density. She was a powerfully built woman, like an Olympic shot-put thrower, but probably weighed as much a slag heap of pig iron twice as big as her. This was a great soldier to have with you when something—living or not—needed to be knocked out of the way or flattened completely.

Thus it was Junebug who got the call from Sarge to get the trapdoor open by leaping onto it as hard as she possibly could. Her weight and momentum coming down from a jump would apply maximal force to the center of the 1.5-meter square, which on this side looked like it was made from the same wood as the rest of the structure. Maybe it was metal on the other side, but there was no way it could withstand this force unless it was reinforced from below by a foot of concrete. Since it would have to be moved out of the way each time anyone or anything went in or out, a concrete or rock barrier seemed unlikely.

"All right, sidearms out and charged," Sarge ordered, and everyone except Junebug, standing in the center of the trapdoor, had their gun out in less than two seconds. "Junie, you're probably gonna break right through and fall all the way down, however far that is. If you can get your arms straight out, punch against the walls and lock your elbows. Same with your legs and knees."

"What if it's too wide?" she asked, not in a whiny way but seeking instruction.

"I've never seen a tunnel made one centimeter wider than it had to be. If there is a tunnel going down, I guarantee it ain't an ass hair bigger than this door."

Junebug smiled at that and said, "Just tell me when to jump."

"And you'll say *How high?* That makes a platoon leader proud, soldier. Keep your comm open and get your sidearm out the instant you stop falling. *Go!*"

Our second assassin crouched and got all her dense bulk balanced to jump and break through the suddenly very weak-looking door. She crouched lower and jumped as hard as she could—

—and the wooden trapdoor broke in two from the force created just by her pushing off.

She didn't gain any height from her jump, instead shooting straight down with all of us watching from a foot or two away. We got a glimpse of the vertical shaft, enough to see that there were handholds on its side and that the room beneath was less than ten feet below us.

Then another door slid into place in the blink of an eye, cutting us off from Junebug.

"Report!" Sarge shouted into his comm. "Junebug, *report!*"

"I'm here, sir!" our comms sounded, and we almost cheered out loud. "But I've fallen into some kind of—" An electronic whine threatened to burst our eardrums and the lot of us—except Sarge—reflexively yanked out our earpieces.

It took a moment for us to see Ernie unconscious on the floor of the gazebo, a moment during which Sarge practically screamed into his comm for Junebug to *report, goddamnit!*

She didn't report.

Ernie was okay after having his Enhancement—which, after all, is coded into his DNA—overloaded with the signal noise. But once he recovered his faculties and had tested his Enhancement to make sure it was still effective, he could find no radio trace of Junebug.

"What *is* this place?" Killshot muttered aloud.

"Motivating," War Thug growled in a voice that chilled us all to the bone.

***

The gazebo was clearly not safe, but its tranquilizing effect kept us there while Sarge decided—with input from each SEAL, but the decision was his alone—what to do next. He couldn't give two Sirius plant pellets about the soothing feeling put out by the structure, but it at least seemed to be a defense against the tremendous Xenos that had taken Inman, so he had us remain encamped there.

Dahlia, despite sharing a name with a gentle flower, was pretty solid herself, so Sarge had her try to jump on the new trapdoor as

Junebug had, only with all of us holding her by the arms and waist to keep her from falling through.

The door didn't budge.

"Ernie, contact the nearest Council base. Tell them I request permission to terminate with extreme prejudice any aliens threatening our platoon or the scientists we're here to rescue. Put me on the comm with them if they give you any flak."

Ernie acknowledged the order and moved to the far side of the gazebo to minimize background noise. (War Council representatives routinely disconnected with any transmission not perfectly clear, as this might be a terrorist trying to pick up military communications and missing by just one frequency point, which would cause static that sounded much like background noise.)

He must have made a good connection, however, because soon he was speaking in official tones, apparently interrupted by his interlocutor several times, and finally sounding exasperated. He turned to Sarge and said, "They say no. No flak, no beating around the bush. Just *no.*"

Sarge shook his head. "Bunch of 'tards over there, I swear to god. Patch me in."

Ernie mentally connected Sarge with whoever was on the other side of the subspace transmission. "Who is this?" he barked immediately. "This is"—he used his real rank and name, shocking us to dizziness—"and I request permission—"

None of us were patched in on the conversation—not even Ernie, who now was merely routing it—but we could see Sarge's face set into an even grimmer visage.

"No, I do not, sir. But—" (I later learned what the other party— a political officer and War Council bigwig—said. It was "Do you have the Council's *eyes only* documents explaining this mission?")

"No, I am not, sir. But—" ("Are you acting in accordance with your sworn duty to execute the War Council's assignments *to the letter?*")

"Yes, sir." ("Are you still interested in commanding a platoon, *War Thug?*")

A pause. "Yes ... sir." A sigh of defeat, then "Understood." ("Then get off the radio and get your ass to work, or I'll find a commander who will, one who does not oppose Council orders and thus *is not a traitor giving aid to the terrorists by such opposition!*")

"*Sir.*" ("Understood ... *what*, commander?")

Ernie said, "Transmission was terminated, Sarge."

"Thank you, comm." Sarge went slowly to a bench and sat, his fist curled under his chin like Rodin's *Thinker*. "Gentlemen, the aliens on Planet Bunghole are officially more valuable than this platoon of Space Navy SEALs. We may not fire upon the Xenos, even in defense. To do so will be considered mutiny against the *Blue Celeste*."

"Against *you*, sir?" Calico asked in a shell-shocked voice.

"No," he said. "If anyone kills one of these *things*, I'll be considered a mutineer as well."

No one made any response to that. One by one, we remaining platoon members took seats on the gazebo benches as Sarge had.

"Troops, I'd appreciate your assistance in getting to these whitecoats and possibly getting our comrades back. I want to do it with the utmost urgency, because then we can get off this rock and back to it."

"To what?" Leonard asked.

"Killing every goddamned thing in sight."

***

Because Ace up in the ship has aimed the space elevator cable almost perfectly, we'd identified the gazebo as being the marker for where the whitecoats' subterranean facility. Now that we took a moment to think of it, however, we realized that we had no confirmation or even evidence that the scientists themselves—if they were even alive—hadn't moved to a different location once their facility was overrun with those waxy seven-foot aliens. Even though they were smaller than those ten-foot behemoths that apparently liked to kill *them*, the tallow-colored Xenos were certainly big and powerful enough to kill three humans without even exerting themselves.

Ernie said, "I continue to detect only automated or other very regular electromagnetic activity from below the gazebo, so I assume the whitecoats are either dead or gone."

"And our men?" Sarge asked.

"Permission to speculate, sir." Ernie cleared his throat a little. "Further, I mean."

"That's all I can ask, unless you've been outfitted with a clairvoyance Enhancement."

Ernie smiled, but after a moment said, "If our people are down there, every bit of their electronic gear has been destroyed or otherwise shut down completely. I'm not picking up even any hum of gear in hibernation mode, sir."

"Conclusions?"

"I think they've moved, maybe to an electronic dead zone down there, or maybe too far from us for their equipment to be detected through all of the closer automated EM noise."

Sarge chewed on this for a moment. "Boz, gimme a rundown on what elements of the team we've lost."

I was certain that he knew *exactly* what the score was, but he sometimes asked for a recap from me to keep the others fully up to date. Nothing this serious, of course, because we as a platoon had never seen anything so FUBAR before as four of our people gone missing. So I went down the list: "From infantry, we've lost touch with Hog and Fugly"—I refused to speculate out loud that we had *lost* any of our teammates—"so we don't currently have their vibration and glamour Enhancements. One assassin, Junebug, is also incommunicado, so her density Enhancement can't be used in a fight or raid situation. And of course the position of Inman, with his Enhanced hearing, is currently unknown."

"That's the real killer," Killshot muttered, and immediately snapped into a rigid standing position. "Sir, I made a remark stating that some of our platoon is more valuable than the rest. I regret this remark, commander and everyone else on this team."

To a person, we all made some gesture or mumbled something to the effect of "Don't worry about it." Sarge, however, stood and positioned himself in front of Killshot, and our sniper kept his eyes forward, not even blinking.

"Dahlia!"

"Sir!"

"Should I punch Killshot in the nose for denigrating your abilities and that of your fellow SEALs?" Sarge didn't move a millimeter from Killshot's face.

Dahlia remained silent as she looked to the rest of us for some guidance, but we didn't have a thing. We'd never seen Sarge do this before. We were usually just chewed out or assigned some pain-in-the-ass duty on-ship that no one ever wanted to do. But not this. Was Sarge thinking mutiny already?

"Dahlia, I asked you a question."

"Sir, I don't think that would be wise, as it would interfere with his visual Enhancement and therefore jeopardize the mission. Also, sir, he denigrated himself along with the rest of the sur—ah, with the rest of us, *sir*."

She almost said *survivors*. The rest of the *survivors*.

Sarge leaned down until Killshot could see nothing but his commander's eyes. Then he said, "You're an asshole. But try not to be *such* an asshole, soldier," and clomped him on the side of the head.

Killshot looked like he was about to puke with relief. And Sarge turned on his heel to face the rest of us … and winked.

That son of a bitch made us laugh in the middle of the worst situation we'd ever faced. War Thug knew how to get every ounce from the people under his command, and even Killshot was laughing now, breaking the horrid tension that came from not knowing if our mates were alive or dead, and if alive, where in hell they could be.

Now we concentrated—because we *could* once again concentrate without being overwhelmed by distress—on how exactly to find them, rescue them and the scientists, and get off of Bunghole. We worked out how we might fulfill this mission and do it without killing a single alien, which would earn our whole platoon the court-martial (and execution for treason) that would follow.

***

We stayed in the gazebo for a few more minutes in order to plan. Sarge called on Leonard first: "Forget that this is impossible. Gimme your plan."

"Um, we should have Ace shoot some pics of the immediate area and see if we can find some alternate entrance or exit to the whitecoat facility. We proceed to that spot and force entry, save the day, and so forth."

"All right, good," Sarge said. "Ernie, relay that to our pilot, please." Now he pointed to Killshot and said, "What you got, everybody's favorite asshole?"

Our sniper allowed himself a small smile, then returned to the task at hand: "Sir, I don't think we've done everything we can to try to open that trapdoor. We went brute force with Junebug, and got shut out again. It must open, because we saw the smaller Xeno drop down after—we have to assume—the rest of its surviving group. Also because that seems the only way Fugly could have been taken during the night from a guarded gazebo she was in the middle of."

Now that he mentioned it, I could see maybe we had given up on the trapdoor too fast, frustrated by the sudden disappearances. The others seemed to agree.

"All right, good. Any suggestions on how exactly we should try to get through it?" Sarge wasn't being sarcastic—he was always open to his troops' ideas and went with them over his own if they were better than his. "Anyone?"

Leonard said, "I could route the plasma blasts from our sidearms on a single spot on the door, try to burn it open or weaken it to try breaking through again."

"But not by jumping on it," Sarge said.

"Agreed."

"Gunner, you're up. What should we do at this point? Just gimme whatever you got."

"I think we should go after those big bastards that took Inman. Killshot was right that his Enhanced abilities are missed already—it sure would be nice to know if there's any sound or movement out there—but as our ordnance man, Inman might also be able to know how to use our weak-ass weapons to bring the Xenos down," Gunner said. "I wish we had brought the railguns, at the very least."

"Why? So we can *not* kill things with them?"

Gunner rubbed his forehead. "Sorry, Sarge. I forgot that part."

Dahlia said, "Well, we could still use the railguns to blast that trapdoor open, with projectiles rather than just plasma—"

"Troops, we don't have the goddamn railguns," Sarge snapped. "You know we can't execute a drop like that, either, so let's focus on what we *do* have, all right?"

"Aye, sir," most of us said. Sarge was right, of course: Ace would have to find some way to secure eight or more heavy railguns to allow them to freefall as a unit, if he could even attach a space elevator clip to them; automate a chute to keep the rifles from smashing into the surface at terminal velocity, making them explode into useless shrapnel that could kill us on the ground; and finally do all this without being sucked out of the ship when he opened the bay for the drop. This last was unlikely, as Ace knew enough to follow protocol and secure himself before opening the aperture around the giant cable. However, if something did happen to Ace—even if he *had* prepared for the unlikely event of falling out by putting on a clip and a chute and survived the unexpected drop—none of us would be returning to the *Blue Celeste*. If we were lucky, Ernie could raise the Council base and ask for rescue. He could *ask*. However, FUBAR missions did not put their crews in the best light with the War Council, and more than one platoon had been left to rot and die on a distant planet.

"Ernest, any ideas?"

"Not unless Gunner brought some grenades with him."

Gunner shook his head ruefully. "Sorry, guys."

"You followed your orders, soldier," Sarge said and turned to Dahlia with a fatherly smile. "*You're* usually full of ideas, Miss Unbreakable. Sometimes I let you have your way just to keep you out of my goddamn face. But tell me you got something for us now."

"I say we give the trapdoor one more shot—blasts, jumping up and down on it, whatever— then follow the giant Xenos to wherever they took Inman *and get him back*. It can't be coincidence that whatever is under that door is taking our troops *and* the Xenos carried our mate away without killing him in front of us. *Something* is going down, and we need to find it until they get all of us and there's no one left to rescue our sorry butts."

Sarge chewed on that, and most of us nodded. Dahlia had laid it all out for us, and there really weren't any other possibilities. We had to fulfill our mission, which was to evacuate the scientists if they were still alive. But us grunts knew that we also needed to know what happened to our mates and get them back to the ship. Dead or alive, they needed to come with us.

"Permission to add something, sir," Calico said.

"Add away."

"I believe there's a good chance that wherever Junebug and Hog and Fugly disappeared to, and we agree that the gray Xenos took Inman probably to the same place, then there's a likelihood that our three whitecoats are there as well."

Sarge nodded, taking it in. "That would certainly be convenient."

"One-stop shopping, sir," Calico said with a tiny smile.

"Okay, assholes, we got two options—" Sarge started, but the rumble of running feet rose from the wooded area so fast that he didn't get to finish. We all turned to look and saw seven of the jaundiced-looking aliens come hauling ass right toward the gazebo we were occupying.

They must have been the same ones as the day before, but they looked a little different: their arms, impressively muscled (in human terms) when we first saw them, now seemed *expanded*, the muscles bigger, the arms much thicker to go with those overdeveloped legs. If they had looked like they could take a human apart yesterday without breaking a sweat, now they looked as if they could do it like cracking an egg.

Those of the platoon who were sitting jumped to their feet; those who were standing whirled practically *en pointe* to face the alien assault. Plasma guns were unholstered. I and, I think, some of my mates puffed up our chests to look bigger, like we were trying to dissuade an attacking bear. But the yellow Xenos didn't break stride and were closing in on the gazebo fast.

"They don't look fierce, commander—they look *scared*," Killshot spat out loudly, and of course he could see them in detail before the rest of us. "Correction: their faces look like scared human faces, sir."

"Understood," Sarge barked, and leveled his plasma gun for when they would enter its range. "They *should* be scared, sons of—"

Sarge cut himself off again now, because a hundred yards behind the smaller Xenos came their enormous fellow natives, the ten-foot gray monsters. "Aw, crap. Killshot, what do *their* faces say?"

Our sniper used his Enhanced vision to evaluate the giants; after a moment, he lost color in his face and stammered, "They're ... *grinning*, sir. Or they look like what a human—

"Got it," Sarge said. "Prepare to fire."

"Fire?" Calico almost squeaked. "But we can't—"

"We can't *kill* them with these pea shooters, but maybe we can make them reconsider."

"Aye, sir," she said, and took aim with the rest of us.

The Yellows were almost to us now.

"I have an idea, sir!" Gunner shouted.

"No time—just make it happen!"

Gunner shoved his pistol back into its holster and leapt running out of the gazebo—*toward the waxy Xenos*.

"What in hell—?" Dahlia said to herself, but also to all of us through her comm, and I'm sure it was the same thought the rest of us had right then. It definitely was mine.

"He's gonna use the calm touch," Leonard said. "Crazy Enhancement touch!"

"I thought that only worked on humans," Killshot said.

"Can it, assholes," Sarge grumbled. "Here we go."

Gunner met the leading yellow Xeno a few yards outside our plasma's reach and just held his arms out to it. The alien's five mates ran past without a pause and in seconds the big and heavy creatures threw themselves into the gazebo, shoving the rest of us—even Dahlia, even *Sarge*—out of the little structure and onto our asses on the other side.

We stood but remained in contact with the gazebo's wood as instructed by our commander as he righted himself. The idea was that we could use the place's "calming field"—all of us had been "calmed" by Gunner before, but the gazebo calmness felt like more of a high than just a lack of tension—to keep the ten-foot Grays away, since they seemed to dislike whatever was being put out from the place.

It seemed that we needn't have worried. Slinking along the edge of the gazebo to get to the side where we could face Gunner and the aliens, we saw that the monsters had ceased to give chase, and in fact had backed off a bit after coming to a halt.

Once we got into a viewing position, we saw what had stopped the giants: The remaining yellow, the one that Gunner had run to and who had not run into the gazebo, had the head of our weapons man in the crook of his elbow, all those now-tremendous muscles ready to break Gunner's neck. The huge Xenos skid to a halt like they had come to the edge of a cliff.

The ten-footers had been grinning as they ran after the terrified small aliens, but now the *Grays* were the ones looking afraid. Not running-away afraid, but don't-move-or-he'll-jump afraid. A trying-not-to-set-off-the-bomb afraid. Obviously, the giants were being held at bay by the yellow's clear threat to separate Gunner's head from his body.

I could see Gunner placing an open palm against the bare waxy skin of his captor, between the straps of its unitard. "He's doing the calm thing," I commed in a low voice.

"As long as he has a head," Killshot said.

"Can it, assholes." Sarge looked like he was exploding into a rage-fueled run and yet standing completely still at the same time, like a powerful engine revving with the brakes on.

"The Xeno doesn't seem any different," I said.

"Maybe its 'calm' is different from ours. Maybe it makes it more confident or something," Calico whispered.

"Or maybe Gunner's Enhancement just doesn't work on—"

"I said *can that chatter*, soldiers," Sarge snapped.

We were standing as a cluster to one side of the wall of the gazebo, with the yellow implacably squeezing Gunner in a headlock yards in front of the opening on that side, the tremendous, muscle-bound Grays holding themselves back. They obviously wanted to twist the smaller alien's head off, but apparently *really didn't want* the smaller alien to do that to Gunner.

We had been keeping all of our attention focused on the standoff, to the point where we didn't notice—

"They're gone!" Ernie gasped, and we all looked where he had his head pointed, which was at the now-empty gazebo. "Sons of bitches opened the hatch and slipped down while we were distracted!"

"Thank you, comm, that's enough," Sarge said, but I could hear the annoyance in his voice that he had allowed us to become so enraptured with what was happening to Gunner that we missed a golden opportunity to get through that door.

Then the yellow Xeno *spoke*. Since the Terran War, no alien species, bug or sentient, had been found to enunciate anything *near* Terran Standard, or TS. The sounds that actually came out of the alien's mouth sounded like he was choking on honey poured down his windpipe, but the words seemed unmistakably like TS as he backed toward the gazebo opening:

"KKhiii wchiiill nakkkkt khhhhhiiill chhhhhhhiiimmm iccccffff ychooo stkkkhaaaay bhhhahk."

I will not kill him if you stay back. That is what we whispered to one another over the comm, to see if this had really happened or whether we were just going insane. Did he say "I will not kill him if you stay back" to the giant Grays? It sure as hell sounded like it.

For their part, the ten-footers seemed to understand, some even to nod, but the sounds they made were like glottal stops between meaningless exhalations of breath. They did stay back, seeming to accede to the yellow's demand and accept his bargain.

The seven-foot Xeno quickly now backed up onto the three wooden steps of the gazebo, Gunner still held tightly by the neck, and—

"*Halt right there! STOP!*" Sarge shouted at the top of his lungs at the alien, who took two more fast backward steps onto the trapdoor, which then opened, dropped him and Gunner inside, and slid closed before any of us could even reach the first step.

Ernie switched off the comm feed as War Thug rumbled into the structure and pounded the closed portal for all he was worth, screaming profanities that seemed to stretch into infinity.

The door didn't budge.

The comm was flicked back on. "Sarge, comm here."

Our commander seemed to pop back into the situation from a place of anger far, far away. "Go, Ernie."

"They're leaving."

Sarge jumped to his feet—really amazing considering the size of his arms and legs, which were small compared to even the yellow Xenos but were *huge* for humans—and actually yelled "*Charge!*" as he pointed his meaty paw after the Grays. The big aliens were making for their open spot in the trees, and all of us immediately went into an all-out run as soon as Sarge gave the order.

It was good that we weren't weighed down with rifles or any gear other than rations, some flak armor, and the card-deck-sized survival kits, because we had to haul ass across that clearing to even keep the slowest gray Xeno in sight. The monsters tromped off before we could even get to the trees—running on two massively powerful legs gave them an advantage not even taking into account the long strides of a ten-foot creature.

We did see that they veered left, however, and that was all we knew when we reached the edge of the clearing. If Inman were still with us—holy god, with Gunner taken *five* of us were gone now— we could've used his hearing to get a better bearing, but we didn't. We had to "SEAL up," as Sarge would say, and keep going without our missing comrades' special abilities.

A rolling rumble of thunder sounded from far away, but not so far that we couldn't see a storm was moving in. On Sarge's order, Ernie commed up to Ace for a summary of weather conditions for Planet Bunghole.

"The atmosphere is a lot like Terra's, but the storms are a little different. Maybe because of the planet's rapid rotation, but it looks like the storms on L-22233 are highly productive of lightning, much more than on Terra," Ace said, and we could all hear it in our comms.

"How long before this one arrives at our location?" Sarge asked, calm but still seething at both varieties of asshole aliens on this planet.

"Fifteen minutes, I'd say."

"Thank you, pilot. We—"

"One more thing, sir. This rock rotates *fast*—you had a seven-hour night, and the six-hour day is about to end. The terminator line will reach you not too long after the storm."

"Great." Sarge turned to Leonard, who had been itching to get our plasma guns routed through his electricity Enhancement the whole time we were in this field. "You hear about the lightning?"

Leonard grinned. "I definitely heard, sir."

Sarge gave a single chuckle and said, "Well, we find those overgrown bastards, you can play with the bolts all you want to get them to take us where we need to do. But Leonard ..."

"Sir?"

"*No killing*. Understood?"

With a smile much diminished but not all the way gone, Leonard nodded. "Understood."

To the rest of us, Sarge barked, "Let's give Leonard a reason to live—let's find those ginormous goddamn things. We got fifteen minutes, platoon."

"*AYE, SIR!*"

* * *

It turned out not to be very difficult to follow the path of the Grays, because there was a ten-foot-high gouge through the canopy of weird alien foliage the whole way. That didn't make it any shorter to get to where they had gone—it seemed like we were double-timing for hours—but it kept us from bickering about which way to go. (It happened on almost every bug hunt when the little vermin—or big vermin—gave us the slip.)

Running across the worn, trampled grass and roots was an occasional indigenous, disgusting four- or six- or twelve-legged Xeno. Dahlia was short of breath as she asked Sarge, "Can we kill these bugs?"

"Negative," Sarge said, not sounding any different than he did when standing still. "The Council could string us up due to a technicality about their *don't kill the aliens* instruction. We fark up any part of this mission, we could become an example for other platoons. And we do *not* want that."

"Roger that, sir." She sounded slightly disappointed, but more winded than anything else.

We followed the Xeno sign for almost twenty minutes before the crashes of thunder and flashes of lightning were upon us. It started to rain, which didn't bother us so much as it made it difficult to see the broken branches and other signs that the big aliens had come through here. The lightning was too random to get a clear view of them, and soon we found ourselves in a clearing, the rain and dark clouds reducing visibility to two meters or so, and night would be upon us very soon. So not only had we lost the trail of the Grays, but now we were all exposed to the heavy lightning that could end any or all of us in an instant.

Sarge yelled through the chaos, "Leonard, engage, if you don't mind!"

I could see Leonard just at the edge of visibility from me. He put out his long arms—and if I hadn't already known the right arm was artificial, I would never have been able to tell. But he stripped off the prosthetic's flesh-like shell and wiggled his spindly automail fingers, real on one hand and metal on the other, into the air above him and yelled, "Everybody stand back and enjoy the show!"

Two seconds after he said that—and you'd better believe we all started moving back immediately—a magnificent lightning bolt slashed out of the sky, made a connection with the right hand of his Enhanced lightning-rod body, and immediately was routed heavenward through his left, back into the oppositely charged storm clouds. To all of us, of course, it looked like *two* lightning bolts had struck him simultaneously, but that was because we couldn't process things moving at the speed of light. Not even

Killshot, with his Enhanced sight, was quite able to do the *completely* impossible.

Another bolt ran through Leonard's body, and another, and another. In just a few seconds, it was practically a constant coursing of electricity through our mate's body. The constant shriek and crash of thunder left us unable to hear Leonard laughing, but the area was now sufficiently illuminated that we could see his face. The man enjoyed his Enhancement, that was for sure.

The light showed much more than our mate's laughter, however; the cycle of lightning—and it seemed like every bolt in the storm was attracted to Leonard—made everything so bright that we could see the entire clearing in almost unbroken clarity. We all looked around for anything that might tell us which way the giant aliens had gone, but Killshot saw what we needed first.

"Sarge, there's a doorway in that mound!" he yelled into the comm, and we all turned to look. "It's metal, sir!"

We all knew what he was getting at—the stuff that was apparently wood in the floor of the gazebo seemed impossible to penetrate. But here was *metal*, and as long as this storm was going on, we had in Leonard a way to direct something as hot as the surface of the sun to melt it.

"He won't see it from there. I can't see it from here and we're a lot closer. Calico, get over there and light up that door with plasma. It won't be hot enough to do anything to it, but it'll make it visible to our mate there."

"Aye!" she barked and took off running in the general direction of where Killshot had identified the mound and door.

Sarge yelled into his comm, "Leonard! Leonard, we need you to aim the lightning at the plasma flashes! *Leonard!* Acknowledge, goddamnit!"

Ernie said over the din, "The flow of electricity is knocking out his comm, sir. He can't hear you or respond."

"I volunteer to go to him, sir!" Dahlia, our unbreakable infantryman, shouted, and at Sarge's nod, ran as fast as she could toward Leonard and the lightning blasts.

"People, get your asses out of the way between Leonard and that door!" Sarge yelled, and we all moved to the side, even though none of us had yet seen the mound Killshot was talking about, either. It was enough to follow our sniper's lead, however, as he backed up double-time.

The rain lessened as Dahlia scrambled to get close enough to Leonard to give him Sarge's order, but that wasn't good news—when the rain stopped, the lightning would stop as well. And Leonard couldn't *create* electricity, just route it any way he wanted.

Which was all we needed.

She got to him, shielding her face from the heat, and we could see her screaming right in his ear. He moved his left hand—the one shooting *out* the bolts—to point it at the distant plasma flashes from Calico's sidearm against the metal door, and then the horrid spectre of FUBAR saw its opportunity and jumped right onto our asses.

The incoming lightning had not ceased flowing through Leonard's right arm, and as he moved the arm directing the also-continuous *outgoing* electricity, the bolt latched onto the nearest conductor—the flesh and blood of the nearby Dahlia—and then into the ground around her, which galvanized her in place as she burned.

Her scream carried over the thunder, and Leonard immediately cut his connection with the storm's electric fury and rushed to her aid as the current released her to fall to the ground. The rain had ceased, and a large majority of the thunder and lightning now was traveling away with the storm. We had lost our chance to melt the mysterious door. If it ever could have been melted.

The rest of the platoon followed Sarge's lead in racing to our mate's location, and it was much worse than I believe any of us could have expected: the right half of her face was charred to red and black, *melted* like plastic left on top of a furnace. Her left foot was apparently where the bolt exited her body and went into the ground; it looked like a piece of chicken that had been baked into blackness.

She wasn't coherent, but she was awake, which was a good sign, I thought. She writhed and screamed and whimpered—so strange to see our stolid mate hurting like this, since her Enhancement allowed her to bounce back practically immediately from any injury—and Ernie fished out his opiate spray to apply on her burns.

"Is this the kind of thing she can heal from?" I asked.

Ernie was our make-do medic, but he gave a gesture that said the answer was beyond him. Sarge nodded and said, "Even if she can't do *her* healing, we'll get her somewhere that she can heal regular."

"We're abandoning the mission?" Ernie asked. "It's all of us go up on the elevator or just one can, and that's it."

"I'm aware," Sarge said, not censuring our radioman for reminding him of something everybody already knew. If it was offered as honest help, he never dressed us down for stating the obvious. "No, we're not abandoning the mission. If that's another entrance to the whitecoats' lab, they got to have some kind of med station."

He looked into the distance toward the mound and metal door that Killshot had pointed out, and now we could all see it, even in the rapidly fading twilight. It was a tall door, but looked foreshortened from our viewpoint because it was angled 45 degrees in our direct line of sight. We had no other hypothesis to go on than that was where the humongous Xenos had gone, and so a tall door opening to stairs or something made more sense than a short, human-sized door.

However, the giants couldn't even speak—if, indeed, that was what the yellow alien did. Pareidolia might have made us hear words where there were only choking grunts, and immediately relevant words as well. That said, if we went with the idea that the bigger aliens were less intelligent than the smaller ones, we doubted they would be able to make and build a door of any kind, let alone a metal one, let alone one leading to some underground facility.

No, I bet the door was built by humans to accommodate the giant monsters. Which raised a lot more questions than it answered, so I didn't bring it up. It wouldn't have been helpful.

It turned out everyone came to that conclusion the same time I did, anyway.

We had all followed Sarge's gaze as he looked at the mound and door, and when we looked back down at our poor Dahlia, the skin had grown back on her face. It was scarred to hell right now on that side, and her hair was gone there too, but the bloody and blackened mess than had been her face just two minutes before had already transformed into undamaged tissue. Same with her destroyed foot. She smiled at Sarge's amazement.

"That is one hell of an Enhancement," he said, and held out his hand to let her stand up.

Her left boot had been reduced to smoking shreds, so she slipped off the other and said, "Sir, permission to requisition new boots upon return to the ship."

"No, just one boot. Your other one seems fine." We all laughed at that, the laugh of tension released. "Now let's see how we can …" His smile vanished in a flash.

"Sir?" I said almost immediately, trying to help him not overload on everything by shifting some of the burden of remembering and keeping logistics straight onto myself.

"Where's Calico?" he said with a voice full of worry.

We all stopped talking or even moving, maybe even *breathing*, in the instant before everyone—including the shoeless Dahlia—ran hell-bent for leather toward the mound half a kilometer away.

"She's got ninja abilities, sir—she might just be hiding," I managed to say as we ran.

At that, all of us to a man started shouting her name, shouting *loudly*. Ernie tried again and again—even as he was running—to raise our assassin on the comm, but her mic and vidcam feeds had completely vanished, just as those of the other missing troops had. No static, no interference, just *gone*.

By the time we got to the mound and its ten-foot-tall door, we had not seen or heard any sign from Calico. She wasn't hiding, she hadn't slipped into the shadows. She had been taken like the others, and we all knew it was through the metal door right in front of us. No handles or knobs, just solid metal with a line down the middle where the two sides met, like on an elevator back on Terra.

It was full dark now, and the moons weren't over the treetops yet. The only light came from our shoulder-mount beams. We banged perfunctorily on the metal for a few minutes, and then my beam flashed over something that Killshot caught notice of. "Boz, look," he said, and adjusted to shine his beam on the spot.

It was a small circle, no bigger than an eyeglass lens, etched into the metal of the door. "Holy sh—Sarge! You want to see this, sir!" Killshot called.

Our commander, who had been only about four feet away but had been doing his best to concentrate his pounding on the door to one spot for maximum damage, stepped over to us and looked at the etching in Killshot's mounted beam. I couldn't see his face, but

I could hear his expression through the set jaw of a man who had been through just about enough: "Fall in for chow. Nobody is to set up his mattress, eat, or even *sit* on this side of the dirt pile. *No one* is to go near that door alone, and *no one*, alone or in a group, is to go near that door, *period*."

To a person, we all made our way around to the doorless side of the pile of dirt and grass. I don't know if the others saw what made Sarge immediately call it a day, but Killshot and I did:

Etched into the metal of the door was the alien insignia.

***

Planet Bunghole's "day" was only six hours, its night just seven. So we lay on our survival beds staring up at stars arranged in constellations we couldn't recognize, and we could see them moving as the Terra-sized planet whirled on its axis twice as fast as our home rock. There were just six of us left: Me, Sarge, Dahlia, Ernie, Killshot, and Leonard. We had our comms off and our body armor plates set aside.

"Platoon," Sarge said, "you assholes have permission to speculate, guess, worry, I don't know—pray to whatever local deity crapped out this galaxy, whatever. I have come to the conclusion that we are not in control of this situation. Therefore, you are welcome to share any serendipitous insights and hare-brained schemes. I want to hear them all; I ain't judging."

"So, like, brainstorm?" Leonard suggested.

Sarge huffed a chuckle. "Sure, yeah. Throw everything you got in there. Kitchen sink, sonic shower—gawd, I could use a goddamn shower—any household gewgaw you want, throw it in there. Nothing could be stupider than what the Council gave us for this mission."

Everyone fell silent, except for Dahlia's gasp and Killshot's *very* quiet "Whoa." Speaking out against the War Council, the only entity standing between a safe Terra and the extinction of our species, was grounds for an immediate and permanent loss of rank and sometimes exile to a prison planet or even execution.

"Excuse me, troops. That was inappropriate. Report me if you feel it necessary. Then put it out of your minds, if you please."

No one said a damn word.

"Anyway, carry on," Sarge said, his "apology" concluded. None of us would report Sarge, but anyone who echoed his technically treasonous sentiment would be asking for serious trouble. A thought against the Council was a virus that would spread to infect every member of a platoon, and Sarge's disowning of his own complaint was an effective way to kill it before it got to anyone else.

Leonard spoke first. "I think they're alive. There's just no reason for the aliens to keep taking our people without harming them if they were just going to kill them as soon as they got them underground."

"The big ones looked frickin' *terrified* when that little one threatened to kill Gunner," Ernie added. "If you can call those yellow things *little*."

"So neither Xeno species necessarily wants to kill us," I said. "Or maybe they like to eat us back in their cave, nice and warm and still alive."

"Lovely, Boz," Dahlia said.

"Sorry—the point is, for some reason they don't kill us when they take us," I said.

"They might kill our men the second they're out of our sight," Leonard said. "The thing that grabbed Gunner might have broken his neck by holding tight when they hit the floor twenty feet under that son of a bitch trapdoor."

"In that case, there's nothing to do for him," I said, "or for the others."

Dahlia groaned. "For Chrissake, Boz, keep it together."

"I'm just saying that we should focus on the mission of getting the scientists out of there if *they're* still alive. Fulfilling the objective should also lead us to what happened to our mates. Everything is centered on that gazebo and this door. It doesn't matter who's dead or alive as far as us needing to get in there. If the vanished troops are alive down there, we can get them the hell out. And if they're dead already ... at least we'll know. We can use the elevator to bring the bodies up as well as those of the scientists, if need be."

"You aren't commander on this mission, Boz," Ernie said. "You're not even second-in-command."

"We don't *have* a second."

"Exactly. Just because you stay at Sarge's side night and day, that doesn't mean you're also in charge. You don't get to set the agenda."

"I'm *not* trying to set the agenda. I'm just reminding—"

"We don't *need* reminding, goddamnit!" Ernie voice rose way too high in volume and pitch, and Sarge had to step in.

"Gentlemen, let's do what Dahlia said—keep it together. Keep *us* together. Boswell, what Ernie said is right: you aren't sharing command with—"

"I'm not *trying* to share—"

"*Sailor!*" Sarge snapped. He rarely used that term when we weren't on the ship, and even then only when he was pissed off. "Did you just interrupt me?"

I swallowed and sat up straight so I could face forward. My face flushed and felt hot. Frustrated tears pushed again my eyes to be released. This all happened before Sarge had even finished his question. I was used to being his shadow, his *ipso facto* right hand man and, as log reporter, his confidante. He had never yelled at me specifically and so angrily. "It was an error of judgment, sir," I managed to say without my voice warbling. "I hope you and my platoon-mates will forgive my mutinous action. It was not intended as such."

Sarge grumbled, "All right, Boz, just cut the crap. Making Ernie and me yell would be a great way to attract those big gray bastards. So try not to be such a depressing twat, logman."

"Aye, sir," I said, and lay back down, still tense in body and mind.

"Sarge, do we have to use that word?" our one remaining female soldier said gently.

"Aw, for Chrissakes, Dahlia, don't be a dick," Sarge said, and we all laughed until we were out of breath.

A moment later, Ernie said, "So what *is* the plan, sir?"

"That's what I'm trying to get you assholes to think about instead of bickering like a bunch of retired admirals playing canasta on a goddamned resort planet. How do you see our options?"

Ernie chewed on it for a few seconds, then said, "There's only one option, the way I see it, sir: we knock in that door or blast it or something, but just get inside. Based on what I'm picking up as EM noise from underground, it's one continuous facility from the gazebo near our drop site to this cellar-door–looking metal portal. If we can get in at either point—damn, I wish Hog was here with his vibration Enhancement. He could rattle that damned door off its hinges or its tracks or whatever the hell these doors are connected by."

"Is the thought that the Grays went down through this doorway?" Sarge said.

Leonard chimed in. "The Yellows holding our mates slipped down the gazebo entrance, and the Grays carried them out of our sight but very likely to this door. It seems built for creatures of their proportions. Occam's Razor says this is where they went; it's the simplest solution."

Sarge said, "Do you understand what you're implying, soldier?"

Silence from Leonard for a good twenty seconds, and then: "If the whitecoats are still alive, and if that insignia on all the sentients' unitards match the one etched into this door, which it does ..."

"Yes, tech?"

"That means that the Xenos and the whitecoats are working together, sir."

Sarge sighed as he always did when faced with a baffling but undeniable truth of the situation in the field. "Can you believe that didn't even register with me?"

Leonard said in a facetious tone, "That's what you have *us* for, sir."

"Good point, soldier. Anyone have a theory about why the Xenos are wearing uniforms in the first place, not to mention ones apparently provided by the Science Division?"

Of course! I thought. *That's the SD symbol!* I felt like a moron not putting it together myself. But I did have a hypothesis, and said so: "My thought is that the whitecoats captured and tamed the Xeno predators, or at least conditioned them not to hurt humans. That's where everything adds up—they didn't kill our platoon-mates, but maybe brought them to the scientists because they were trained that the underground facility is a *safe zone*. You run into humans, whom you have ingrained in you not to hurt. There is a designated safe zone—the facility beneath us—and so the Xenos bring our people underground to keep them *safe*."

After a minute, during which everybody seemed to chew this over, Killshot said, "Boz, has your Dad been helping with your homework?"

Everybody laughed at that, and in a way that seemed to acknowledge the validity of my take on things. It felt good, I don't deny it. And then, of course, Sarge slipped a turd into my punchbowl: "All right, Boswell, good thinking. So if the whitecoats have housebroken and trained the aliens to do tricks, why did they send an emergency extraction request to the quadrant Council base? Why do they have that rescue message playing on a loop? My question boils down to *Why are we here*? If they need us and are alive, why the cat-and-mouse garbage?"

I was stuck. I stared at the band of the Milky Way, not so different here than on Terra. We were in a different quadrant, but close enough to home to see the pale yellow of our own sun among the thousands on display in this whirling night sky. So close that subspace messages took seconds instead of minutes to send and receive from Terra. The quadrant Council base, while farther up the galactic arm than we were from the Terran home base, was close enough to us that subspace transmissions were practically instantaneous. (Our ships' drives and all subspace communications exploited a handy feature of Minkowski spacetime that allowed us to dilate space instead of time as we traveled near the speed of light, which meant that we could travel a light-year in less than a minute. It didn't violate Einstein's upper speed limit of travel in our universe, because we never traveled faster than the speed of light. We simply performed a Lorentz transformation in one of the spatial dimensions rather than the single time dimension. It's all very simple if you're an advanced mathematician or physicist, I'm sure, but us grunts on the *Blue Celeste* were just happy it worked. Spending a couple of days traveling in subspace was boring enough—years would be unbearable, not to mention completely ineffective in the War Council's battle against the alien menace. They couldn't have time dilation happening all over the place and platoons returning from missions one hundred years after the threat they were to eliminate had already wiped out the rest of Terra's population.)

In other words, we were far enough from any base to prevent us from even temporarily abandoning the mission and looking for backup or additional supplies or anything; we were on our own. However, we were close enough to the home base and the quadrant base—almost right in the middle, in fact—that they could keep tabs on our mission, practically in real time. We were under extremely strict orders not to kill anything even remotely sentient. The Xenos didn't kill any of our people that we could see, and most of our guys had been taken while the rest of us were otherwise occupied or distracted.

"It's a training mission," I said at last. "This is all a setup from Council Command to test our skills in the field and make sure we're still functioning as a unit at optimal capacity." I listed my bits of evidence, maybe none convincing in itself, but taken as a whole, pretty damned solid.

Sarge huffed, "We've successfully executed, without exception, every mission that this platoon has ever been tasked with. Not a man lost in I don't know how many assignments, and with this crew none at all, ever. We obviously perform at top efficiency, Boswell—why would the Council waste time and money on setting up a goddamn *evaluation scenario* when we have never let a mission go FUBAR in all our years together?"

"Sir, as you always say, all I know is the *what* and all I need to figure out is the *how*. The *why* of anything the War Council tells us to do is none of our damned business."

"Boy, I'll tell ya—never say anything to a memory-Enhanced soldier you don't want brought back up at an inconvenient time," Sarge said, and his ironic tone let me know that my advice and counsel was taken seriously and appreciated, even if he might end up not following it. "How about the rest of you assholes? Is Boswell onto something, or has he lost what was left of his mind?"

There was some murmuring, but Leonard finally said, "It does sound like something our … *superiors* would come up with. They might see continued perfection in action as a smokescreen for something else, like we're executing mission after mission so we don't get audited by the Council with an evaluation scenario and expose our *treasonous secret* or some such. Also, we'd know we were being watched in a scenario—with whatever the heck *this* is, we'd treat it like the real deal, thus do our alleged surreptitious activity in full view of the Council auditors."

"Holy crap," Killshot said.

"Why would they think we're *traitors*, for god's sake?" Dahlia shouted, sitting up and making the rest of us realize we shouldn't be seen all of a sudden as literally lying down on the job. Sarge had never lain down. "We've done nothing but follow orders to the letter, killed everything on entire planets, *liberated* technology for Terra … *it's a slap in the face!*"

"Your emotion is understandable," Sarge said, "but this is war. To say even what you just said is treasonous. Our comms are shut off, but if Council Base heard what you said just now, they wouldn't hesitate to put you to work shoveling salt on M6-117 for the rest of your enlistment and then—when they *forget* to off-world you—the rest of your wasted life."

We were all silent. Every one of us, and it had to be true of every human being who had ever served the Space Navy or under any hierarchical structure, had at one time or another said something critical of the War Council. Even our commander had. Maybe the Council never took action against us because our platoon had a spotless record. But now maybe that very record made us look suspicious, like we were somehow conspiring with the enemy to make it *look* like we had always won.

"It ain't nothing against you, Dahlia. The assumption is and has always been that every Terran outside of War Council members is a potential traitor, trying to weaken the human race's defenses against the rest of the galaxy. As Boswell said, they don't need to explain *why* to anyone, just the *what* of the accusation—with its automatic conviction for being accused, because whatever the Council does is correct—and the *how* of the punishment following your crime." Sarge finished his speech and spat on the ground.

"So what in the hundred systems are we supposed to do now?" Killshot said, sounding very much at the end of his patience with this entire discussion.

"We finish the mission *to the letter*, soldier." Sarge stood now, and the rest of us followed suit. None of us would really have been able to rest anyway. "We extract the scientists and don't worry about a single goddamn thing we've seen here. Getting the scientists out is the *only* objective of this mission."

"But what if they're already dead?" Ernie said, looking a little sick.

"If this is the Council testing our resolve and loyalty, radioman, our men are not going to be dead. Just a bitch to find." Sarge put on his comm unit, and we took that a signal to do the same. Ernie radio-checked us all, and they worked as well as ever, although Ernie had needed to swap out Leonard's lightning-blown unit with a spare. "So, Boswell, you started us down this happy hall of mirrors—what's your plan to get us underground there so we can extract the whitecoats and complete this godforsaken mission?"

"And our other SEALs, right?" Dahlia asked in a tentative quiver. "They won't actually be dead if this is an evaluation exercise, right?"

Sarge didn't answer, especially not after warning us to clam up with any complaints about the War Council did its job. "Boswell, speak."

"I do have an idea, but you're not going to like it, sir."

"Try me."

"We need to put out some bait in order to lure some of the Xenos out here, since they are obviously really good at snatching anyone near their portals. Then we rush in as soon as the door opens and the monsters get out of the way. We can't break through the doors, so the only way is through stealth and trickery."

"You're right, Boswell," Sarge said, "I *don't* like it."

"Oh." *Well, hell.*

"But it's the best anyone's come up with. I think we should make it a go. All those in favor, hold your tongues. Let me hear from those opposed to this plan."

Nobody spoke.

Sarge let a minute or so tick off the clock, then said, "All right, then. Next question for you assholes: Do it now, or wait until first light?"

"Day would be safer, because we could see," Dahlia said.

"Brilliant insight, Dahl," Killshot said.

"Secure that, please," Sarge said.

"Night could be safer because maybe the Xenos can't see well in dark conditions once the moons have gone behind the treeline," Leonard said.

Ernie responded, "But neither can we."

"These are all good observations, people," Sarge said. "No matter when we try it, though, we need someone to act as bait so we can leave one of these bad boys with his pants around his ankles. Or his little yoga suit, whatever. Now, who wants to be our best chum?"

We all groaned at the boss's terrible joke. Then Leonard sat up and said, "I volunteer, Sarge. If the door here and probably at the gazebo too opens and closes automatically according to some signal algorithm, I'd be the person who could fix that or jam it or make it just stay open from the inside. I should be the bait."

"What if they *are* killing their captives?"

Leonard barely even paused. "Then we're all dead anyway. Why not be next?"

"God, you sound like Boz," Dahlia moaned.

"Excellent, Leonard. Here comes the million-dollar question: Now or later?"

"Now," Leonard said. He was raring to go.

"Now," Ernie said.

"Now." Dahlia.

"Now." Killshot.

And, finally, me: "Now."

We sat in a loose huddle and started planning. After a few minutes, Ernie said, "Sorry, sir, but I need to see a man about a Triffid."

"If you're gonna tell me you want to go around that dirt to piss in private, you can friggin' hold your water," Sarge said. "Everybody is sticking together from this moment forward."

"No, sir, just a few yards over this way. Dahlia, don't watch."

"Oh, *pleeease*? Just the first few drops?"

Ernie laughed along with the rest of us and walked off to relieve himself onto the grass. We kept talking about what exactly our fishing plan was going to entail, but I noticed Sarge keeping an eye on our radioman. There didn't seem to be anything around that could snatch him up before one of us could get to him, but if we lost Ernie, we wouldn't even be able to contact Ace in the ship to bring us up.

But if things got that desperate, Leonard was right: we'd all be dead anyway.

Because Sarge was watching Ernie as he had his back to us, he noticed something and sat bolt upright. "Killshot," said with urgency.

"Sir?"

"Stick those peepers on whatever the hell that is about five yards past piss-boy, about two o'clock. What the hell is that?"

Killshot stood, turned, and squinted where Sarge had specified. Even in just the moonlight, I could see our sniper lose a bit of color and his mouth drop open in shock.

"Sir, it appears to be … a head."

***

Sarge wasn't kidding about us sticking together. He wanted to investigate the body-free head lying sideways in the grass, and so we all got up and went as one to investigate. Ernie buttoned up and waiting for us reach him before he got any closer to it as well.

The object on the ground was definitely the part of a body that ideally is found on top of a neck. However, it was yellow and too big for a human head. The obvious conclusion was that this waxy Xeno's head had been twisted off by one of the gray Xenos, just as we had seen when the smaller aliens fell behind in running from the bigger aliens. But …

"Where's the rest of it? I asked, scanning the immediate area like the rest of the platoon. "Don't tell me the Yellows are prey."

"What, do you think they hunt for sport? I don't think they're *that* sentient," Killshot said. "That sumbitch done got et."

Everybody—well, all us grunts—jumped, startled by an abrupt, *loud* screech like the wrenching of metal against metal. It came from the other side of the mound.

The door side.

"*Door!*" Leonard bellowed at the very top of his lungs and started sprinting before he had finished the word. "Got to get in there before it closes!"

Sarge barely had time to register that Leonard was off and running before he unleashed his roar: "*Sailor, get your ass back— Leonard! Goddamnit, CORPORAL WILSON! Get your ass—*"

Our commander was livid with rage, but it was impossible not to detect the fear in his voice as well. But Leonard, whether he heard Sarge or not over the screech of metal, saw something ahead and hit his brakes so fast that he tripped on himself and fell over.

What he saw was a dozen mammoth gray Xenos pouring out from the door side of the mound and rounding the corner to run at us—at *him*, since he had charged without an order. What he couldn't see right away was another eleven of the giants streaming out on the *other* side of the mound. That made *twenty-three* monsters (I didn't count them while they were coming out but rather when I used my recall to enter it into this log report) racing right at our diminished troop of six SEALs. Really five SEALs since one of the massive aliens lifted Leonard like he was a uniform filled with cotton balls and walked—*walked*—back around to steal him underground.

We all saw this, but even more immediate than trying to save our comrade was trying to not end up captured or slaughtered by the Xenos ripping our heads off like they did that poor yellow bastard. They had seemed absolutely opposed to harming us, even acceding to a yellow Xeno's threat to kill Gunner rather than advance on the rest of us or claim the smaller alien's head as a hunting trophy.

We had exactly no seconds until the twenty-two of the rampaging mothers were upon us. Killshot, Ernie, Dahlia, and I whipped out our plasma pistols and fired as many streams as we could manage. The blasts knocked the giants back for a very short moment, but wouldn't be damaging any of them, let alone put them down for the count.

That's when War Thug appeared. It was like he had stripped off his responsible soldier skin and unleashed the beast inside.

With a scream that shook the ground as much as the Gray's thundering footsteps, War Thug grabbed the first giant that reached him, reared back a massive arm (which looked puny compared to the ten-footers', of course) and threw a punch with his massive fist right into the center of the Xeno's chest. The higher pitch of a sternum snapping reached everyone's ears over the lower grunts and stomping of the attack. The rest of the giants took their eyes off of us grunts and saw with shock what had just happened.

The alien that War Thug had punched stumbled backwards a few feet, looking down at the whitish crack in the middle of his chest, between the unitard straps. What appeared to be vomit, although white like the crack where he had been hit, poured from the thing's mouth all down its chest. But still he stood, although he looked like he could be knocked over by a light wind.

Standing wasn't how War Thug wanted him, however. He took two long strides toward the injured alien and threw his powerful fist at the exact same spot as before, which blew the Xeno's chest wide open. There wasn't even time to scream—if these things ever screamed—before War Thug's fist kept going until it reached the alien's heart, which our commander pulled from inside its chest until the sound of rubber bands snapping stopped and the giant thing fell dead to the ground.

War Thug held the white heart in his hand, his face and hands dripping with viscous white fluids. He glared at the remaining Xenos, and took an enormous bite out of it. He chewed as he stomped toward another one of the attackers. The looks on their all-too-human faces showed nothing but shock and panic, and they froze in place, stealing glances at one another's oversized faces for a clue of what to do.

They waited too long.

Just as the remaining big bastards turned about-face and ran for the door they must have left open on the other side of the mound, War Thug took a running leap onto the back of the hindmost alien, which brought him up to about the small of the thing's back, then unsheathed a huge Bowie knife and rammed the point of the curved blade right through the son of a whore, then ripped it out sideways, the laser-honed instrument slashing its way out practically without resistance. The Gray immediately fell to its knees, gushing white gunk, but before it could flop onto the ground, War Thug climbed the body as it collapsed forward and unleashed a huge twist of its head, killing the alien good before it even reached the ground.

None of the rest of us moved, since we had no idea what to do with the giants—Killshot, Dahlia, Leonard, Ernie, and I had useful state-of-the-art Enhancements, but none of them were super-strength or unstoppable fury. So we just watched as War Thug leapt and, keeping his hands stretched as far up as they could go, drove his weapon right through the back of a third retreating monster's head, going all the way through. The weight of the alien pulled the knife from War Thug's hands as it fell all the way to the ground, dead already.

It was taking the time to unstick the curved blade from the Gray's head that saved the rest of the bastards. The remaining seven practically hurled themselves forward to get back to the open door.

It was our golden opportunity to rush the door and get inside, but Sarge yelled at us, "Do *not* follow! Keep your ground, soldiers! We ain't going down there without a plan like a bunch of commissioned asshats."

And he *was* back to being our Sarge, his entire morphology seeming to relax from Human Tank into just regular badass in seconds. He was still coated with white alien blood or whatever that was, but War Thug had crawled back inside our commander's mind, always ready to come out and *kill*. Sarge had guessed right that they had a skeletal structure and heart-type organ that were analogues of our own—cephalic Xenos almost always had a brain in their melon, so that was a very reasonable place to jam his Bowie knife—so the gunk they oozed probably was their blood. Looked more like pus, though.

"*They got Leonard!*" Dahlia cried.

"Secure that right now," Sarge said so firmly I felt my own jaw tighten. "Where is—? Count off, people, *now*."

"Killshot."

"Dahlia."

"Boswell."

We knew we wouldn't hear Leonard's voice, but when Ernie didn't count off …

"Ernie? Comm?" Sarge barked. "Report, comm. *Report, comm!*"

A crackle sounded in my earpiece. "Ernie here, sir."

We all looked in surprise at our leader, who seemed slightly shaken himself. "Ernie, where the hell are you, son?"

"I saw an opportunity and took it, sir. The door didn't shut until a few seconds after the last Xeno ran inside, so I located my balls and slipped in before the moment was lost."

Sarge's sigh sounded more like a groan. He said, "Did you not hear me order everyone to stand fast? I believe I yelled it so loud Ace could hear me upstairs without his comm."

"Sir, I did hear you, but by that time I was five feet from the door and committed to this plan of action. It was not disobedience—I was just *so* close, I couldn't stop myself."

Sarge chewed on this for a moment, checking the rest of us for any reaction. When he saw none forthcoming, he commed to Ernie, "Understood. Good work. Since they didn't capture you, your comm is obviously still working. Give us the situation with the door, please: Can you get it open for us? We'd love to join you."

"Can you see what they've done with Leonard?" Dahlia blurted, then put her hand over her eyes. "Sorry, sir, I—"

"It's all right. I'm sure we all were thinking the same thing. But let's focus."

Crackle. "The Grays ran ahead while I waited for a chance to contact the platoon. I didn't see Leonard at all, probably because he was taken by the first Xeno that came back. I just saw Xeno ass in those goddamn weird outfits. Excuse my language over the radio, Sarge."

"No time for niceties. How about that door? There's gotta be some kind of mechanism to make it open."

"Looking, sir. I wish Leonard were here—a tech could probably figure it out in five seconds."

"Well, what we got is *you*, so think like Leonard. Find a switch or a latch or control panel."

Killshot murmured, "Damn, I wish he had brought the vidcams! Then he could just show us the area, and I bet as a group we could figure it out."

"People, if *ifs and buts* were *cherries and nuts*, we'd all have a Merry Christmas," Sarge growled. "But since our Fairy Godmother ain't showing up, how about we stop with the wishing for five goddamn seconds."

"There's nothing but metal and bolts and such, sir," Ernie said. *Crackle.* "I can see how the doors are opened and closed—basic metal rods, one for each door, but I don't see any wires or buttons or anything."

"All right, soldier. Maybe there's a control panel you'll see as you go. Now, as carefully as you can, go the way you saw the Grays go. It doesn't matter if you take all night, just go slow and do *not* get yourself captured or killed."

Sarge didn't have to say it, but we'd have no way to contact Ace to unhook the space elevator cable and bring us up if we didn't have Ernie's Enhancement of an A/V switchboard in his head. We all knew the situation and the danger. Also, after seeing War Thug put down three muscle-bound Xeno almost four feet taller and twice as wide as himself—one with his bare hands—we grunts agreed that his Enhancement had to be brute strength with super bones, along with an inability to feel pain, or some combination. (We had seen him go on a rampage before and kill tons of aliens using his huge hands or rocks or other items lying about if his blaster weapons malfunctioned or were lost, but I'd never seen him do anything as epic as taking down something so massive as it attacked at a full run, then chasing down two more to end their terrorist careers.)

"Also, Ernie, make note and tell us how far you're inside, if there are any bends or turns, that kind of stuff. We want to walk right above you to make sure there's no loss of our comm link."

Crackle. "Aye, sir."

A thought occurred to me. "The scientists have to be alive, Sarge," I said. "Somebody's got to be opening and closing the doors for these things."

Killshot said, "It could be a weight sensor or some kind of visual recognition software."

"I don't think so. These things have got to weigh a *lot*, but our platoon at full capacity weighs more than one of them, definitely more than the yellow ones. And the software, man—why the heck would the whitecoats set up recognition tech that lets them *in?*"

"Mysteries, my mates, buncha goddamn mysteries," Sarge mused, chewing on what we said as he paced back and forth. Slowly, but it was undoubtedly pacing. That did not inspire confidence, something Sarge would have secured immediately in a less insane situation. "Why this, why that, why the other. It don't *matter why* anyone would do anything—all we need to worry about is why can't an *elite military squad get through a goddamn wooden door*? Why can't this platoon of Space Navy SEALs, who have been together through five tours without losing one man, figure out how to get past a metal door that Ernie says isn't reinforced with *anything?*"

"It's got to be a training exercise or maybe a test, like you said," Dahlia said with a finality I bet she didn't feel. "The Council is giving us the hardest training exercises because we're the best platoon in the quadrant. Some things are gonna look impossible, or make no sense—that's why it's a test. They want to see how we handle a FUBAR situation. Of course, that's just my two cents, sir."

"Thank you, infantry. Either way, if it's a training exercise or test, or if it's a genuine pear-shaped sideways f'ed-up situation, we have to get through those goddamn doors. We don't need to do nothing else, *nothing*. Just get us through that door, soldiers."

Crackle.

"Ernie? Comm, come in."

Crackle-crackle. "Sir, I'm deep in the <crackle> can you <crackle> me?" Our radioman's voice, even through the static and interference, was unmistakably panicked. "It's not what <CRACKLE> was, sir!"

"Ernie!" Sarge shouted as if his voice could be projected through the static by sheer will. "What is happening down there? It's not *what*, soldier? What's your position? *Ernie!*"

A blast of static brought our hands to our earpieces, then Ernie's desperate voice, coming in and out and impossible to make into a coherent sentence: "They're still <crackle> don't come <CRACKLE> normal <crackle> if you don't—"

And with that, we lost the link to Ernie completely. We didn't even get static.

We had been through some hellish battles together, but I had never heard Ernie's voice like that. It was more than frightened or even panicked—he sounded *doomed.*

Like we all were. Because our leader, our mentor, our trusted comrade, had just pissed away all of our jobs and quite possibly the rest of our lives.

"Sir, permission to speak candidly," I said, a little trepidation in my voice.

"I know what you're going to say, logman."

I nodded. I knew he did, but I said it anyway: "We weren't supposed to kill these Xenos."

He sighed hard, and sat down on the grass, his great bulk hunched over and inert. "I'm sorry, troops," he said. "My War Thug tendency just exploded out of me. I couldn't control it. Or maybe I could've, but *I didn't want to.* And now we're all dead men walking. I failed the Council, I failed my platoon, I failed myself. If you three want to strike out on your own when we get brought up, you're welcome to the ship. No sense in offering your necks to be guillotined by the Council. Go find a corner of space and stay there. I'm gonna stay right here."

We had nothing to offer Sarge but our silence. And, after whispering to one another for a few minutes, our renewed loyalty. We would all die together, even if that were at the hands of the Council for failing this test—if it even *was* a test, instead of just a complete disaster of a mission. We might all live, or we might all die, but we would do it as we did everything else.

As a team.

***

Sarge remained sitting cross-legged on the grass at an oblique angle to the mound's metal doors, but after ten minutes or so barked, "Dahlia, Killshot, Boswell, how many times have I told you this platoon is not a goddamn democracy?"

"Many times, sir!"

"Well, Benjamin Franklin just called. We're gonna take a vote."

The three of us grunts stole glances at one another. We were sitting ten yards or so away from Sarge, because he told us he needed a minute to grok "this whole goddamn fustercluck." It wasn't a question Sarge had just put out; it was a statement, even an order. We stood and crossed the distance between us and our commander, giving him the respect of standing at attention while he also stood to address us. This kind of formality meant only one thing: Sarge was going to lay down the law and *tell* us what the plan was now.

However, his calling it a "vote" was unprecedented for the crew of the *Blue Celeste*. He always, *always*, asked for input and opinions on important decisions, but he had never called for or allowed a *vote* on any action we took as a platoon.

"What's on the ballot, sir?" Killshot said.

"We need to strike quick and we need to hit hard to get down into those whitecoats' lab, get our people the hell out of there, and kill the rest of those Xenos whether the Council likes it or not."

We nodded, but Dahlia spoke up first: "Sir, why don't we just get reeled back to the ship on the elevator and drop a Super-Nuke, kill everything on this lousy planet?"

Sarge chuckled mirthlessly. "Dahl, you are a fine SEAL and an excellent crew member, but I swear to god you have a bag of sand where your brain should be."

"Ouch, sir."

"Ah, it ain't you—it makes sense that under extreme conditions, our memories and actions may become questionable or downright ass-backwards," Sarge said, waving away any bruised feelings. "I killed those bastard Grays, and maybe got us all a death sentence. And you forgot that we just lost our comm-Enhanced soldier, so we would have no way to contact Ace up there to bring us up when it was time."

Dahlia closed her eyes, no doubt to feel the burn of forgetting something so important.

"But it's not just that," he continued. "I know if you thought for five more seconds before you spoke, you would remember that there's a good chance our troops are down there and alive. This is going on Killshot's idea that the whitecoats must be alive down there to let the creatures in and out. So we can rescue our comrades, liberate the scientists, and kill the Xenos. If we pull off that central extraction mission, maybe the War Council will let us keep our heads, if not our jobs."

"Understood, sir."

"One more thing, and this is for all three of you assholes: a Super-Nuke ain't something you do to a planet unless you *hate* it. I ain't talking about *I hate aliens on this planet* or *I lost platoon-mates on this planet*. You explode Super-Nuke when you want every sentient, every bug, every tree, every blade of alien grass, every drop of water in the ocean and every molecule of breathable atmosphere on that planet to be scoured away by hellfire. It kills everything—*everything*—but it's even more than that, people. Do you know how exactly a Super-Nuke works?"

"It's not like a Neutron weapon? Or a Death's Head Nuke?" Killshot asked, sounding perplexed and—if he was anything like me right then—scared to hear whatever Sarge was going to say next.

Sarge shook his head slowly, ruefully. "Naw, not like those. A Neutron weapon is used for small, concentrated population centers, cities and such. Kills everything, keeps their tech ready to be seized and copied. And the Death's Head ... it'll render a hemisphere uninhabitable for ten thousand years, but eventually life on the planet is gonna recover.

"But a Super-Nuke? They shouldn't even really call it a *nuke* because it doesn't use atomic chain reactions and all that crap to blow up and spray radiation everywhere. No, a Super-Nuke doesn't explode at all—it creates those chain reactions in the atoms of the drop site itself. And that initial chain reaction, the one that splits the first atom in a regular nuke and makes the fusionable material get converted directly into energy and go *BOOM*? In a Super-Nuke, it creates that initial split of the atom, but not just that one atom—it makes every atom into fusionable material. That means it splits *every* atom in contact with the device when it is activated. That's god knows how many runaway chain reactions with any atoms in the vicinity of the initial multi-quintillion split atoms. *Those* atoms set off a chain reaction with the next set of atoms, and so on, and so on, until every atom on the planet is converted into violent, devastating energy. In other words, the entire planet becomes the bomb. Ain't nothing left of a planet after a Super-Nuke, and that means the whole system is going down, because completely erasing a planet will throw the others out of their orbits, toss them into the central star or fling them into the vast wasteland of space."

It was the longest speech I had ever heard Sarge give, and I felt empty when he had finished. Just as he said, a Super-Nuke wasn't for fumigating the bugs or poisoning the sentients of a planet: It was a weapon of *hatred*, to be used when no part of that planet's existence can ever be anything but a threat to Terra. I cleared my throat and said, "Sir, have you ever seen a Super-Nuke used in the field, or tested? I mean, if there's any way to test something like that and not get killed yourself."

Sarge looked up at me and said, "No, Boswell, I haven't. No one has. I don't think it's ever been used since the Council developed it, except for one *test*, as you call it. From a very safe distance—I'm talking a solar system's width away—they set one off on an uninhabited rock orbiting within the Goldilocks Zone. That vid is transmitted constantly on all subspace and Minkowski spacetime wavelengths not used for military communications. If we make it back, put on your helmet and tune the comm to give you the whole thing on your HUD. Needless to say, it's a hell of a deterrent for any terrorist Xenos who might even *think* about attacking our home world."

"Jesus Christ," Dahlia said.

"At the very least," Killshot answered, his face pale and voice like a dog when it hears its abusive master putting his key in the front door's lock.

"And the War Council don't want it used *ever*, because once it becomes familiar and its effects—no matter how horrible— become fathomable, it will be cast down from the realm of myth and terror into the world of engineering and comprehension. No ship sets off a Super-Nuke unless the Council orders it—and they ain't never gonna order it."

We let all of that sink in—even I, the records and logman for our platoon, had never been briefed on the Super-Nuke. That might have been because they knew that not a single detail would ever be forgotten by their Enhanced-memory man; or it might have been, as I had always deep down believed was the case, that the Super-Nuke was a comforting falsehood, one to make all in the military and back on Terra breathe a sigh of relief that there was *something* that could stop an alien attack once and for all before it even had a chance to start.

Finally, I said, "So what are we voting on, then, sir? Whether to go up on the cable—if we could somehow make contact—or to keep banging away at the doors to the lab until we break through?"

"No, soldier. We're getting down there. I just want a vote on what doomsday scenario we're gonna follow to do it."

No one said a word, but I felt a pinprick of sweat on my forehead. I could hear Killshot swallow loudly before he said, "Aye, sir." A pause. "And the candidates …?"

"Good," Sarge said. "We got two choices, people. One is that we find a way to either bash in, yank out, or somehow pry open the doors' on the mound here. The other is that we make Planet Bunghole a gazebo-free zone by just destroying that whole creepy-ass structure and thus get better access to that trapdoor and whatever is under it. You guys want to caucus, give some pros and cons to your fellow voters? There's three of you, so we can't get a tie."

"Don't you get a vote, Sarge?" Dahlia said.

"I vote that you assholes get a goddamn move on and decide already."

Abashed, Dahlia was the first to announce a decision. "I think we should stay here and keep going at those doors until we can get through or some Xenos come out again. There could be more outside, too, so maybe they'll open the door to get in."

"All right, those are the pros. Cons?"

"The doors might be unbreakable, like Leonard's right arm. Also, we have no idea if more Xenos are gonna be coming by here soon, and we can't wait to strike if we're to have any chance of saving our mates."

We all nodded. She seemed to have that pretty well figured out.

Killshot said, "I vote for the gazebo. Whatever *calmness vibe* it sends out may be destroyed if we take that mother apart. I don't see my … *enthusiasm* for getting our boys back being diminished in the time it will take for us to tear that damned thing to pieces." He looked at waiting for him to continue. "Oh, cons, right — I could be wrong and we *could* be calmed into inaction by the gazebo's vibratory sympathies or whatever. And there's no guarantee we'll be able to get through that trapdoor even with a new angle provided by murdering the gazebo."

More nods. Sarge nodded to me and said, "You're the tiebreaker, Boswell. What say you?"

I knew immediately. "I vote for making that gazebo our bitch."

Sarge laughed with my two comrades and said, "Best argument I ever heard! The gazebo it is." Before we could even start moving in the breaking dawn, Sarge stopped us. "Wait—that's a huge pro, but what are the cons?"

I thought for half a second and said, "Two things. One is that we might run into some of the gray Xenos, or even the yellow. Even if we can kill them to get past, it might delay us too long to save our mates."

"What's the other con?"

"Planet Bunghole offers nothing but danger. There's a distinct chance that the gazebo might make bitches out of *us*."

***

We packed up and compressed our gear as we waited for the L-star—which I now am sure stood for "Luckless"—to rise. Every second was precious, but we needed enough light to allow us to make a fast-cadence march back to our drop site and the mysterious gazebo.

"I wonder what Ace is thinking," Dahlia said as we hiked, not out of breath in the slightest. "Sarge, what's his protocol?"

"Pilot protocol is to wait for an order from the nearest Council base. If that order is to wait, he waits. If it says to leave, then he'll unhook the drop cable, reel it in, and immediately slip into subspace to report to the base."

"Gah, I hope he'll wait for us!"

"I hope he'll do whatever the Council orders him to do. If he doesn't and we get back up there, I'll kick his ass. There's no sense in putting his head on the chopping block next to ours. *He didn't fark up this mission.*"

We were almost at the end of the path leading to the clearing and our target when we heard the unmistakable sound of labored breathing. We barely had to turn our heads to see one of the waxy yellow Xenos, its pinkish blood running in rivulets from bones sticking through skin, lying in the brush not five yards from us.

We halted immediately, none of us able to tear ourselves from staring at the alien, who was in obvious pain and distress. Sarge said to Killshot, "What can you see? Is this a trap or what?"

"Checking, sir." Killshot did his thing, narrowing his eyes to catch every detail of something so close, where the rest of us just saw a yellow form and pink liquid draining from it. "The alien looks legitimately hurt. If its bones are broken like they seem— and that is *everywhere* on the poor bastard, excuse my language— then this Xeno poses no danger to us in itself. But that doesn't mean it wasn't beaten half to death and left here as bait by the Grays."

"Very good, soldier. You assholes remember when we took a vote?"

Of course, we did.

"Well, that's over—Dahlia, get your pistol out and approach the subject. See if it can speak like before. If it ain't safe, get right back here. If it is, call us over. Understood?"

Dahlia unsheathed her plasma weapon. "Understood, sir."

She was infantry, but had also picked up a few techniques from our platoon's assassins. She slinked in sideways—she was a muscled wide woman—using the trees to block the Xeno's view of her until she was in his face, weapon pointed at him with no ambiguity regarding her intentions.

"Speak, yellowface," she ordered, and the alien's human face turned up immediately to take her in. Killshot kept his eyes trained on the encounter and reported to us what was happening, although of course he couldn't hear the conversation like Inman could have.

"Gahrunnnnnnt," the creature breathed out, eyes fixed on Dahlia and her weapon. "Innnfantrrrreee …"

Grunt and *infantry*. Dahlia almost recoiled at the waxy thing's words. "How do you know these words? How do you know—wait, the scientists taught you Standard, didn't they? *What are they doing down there?*"

Killshot said, "That poor son of a bitch isn't going to last much longer, boss."

Sarge acknowledged the information with an affirmative grunt. "Secure the analysis, soldier. Just tell me what you see."

"Aye, sir." He squinted at the scene, which I knew meant he was going for maximum close-up and detail where Sarge and I could only see two people—one person and a dirty Xeno, I mean, of course. "I see Dalia kneeling down to the creature. It looks like it's pulling the front part of its uniform bottom—"

"Gah," I said, earning daggers from the eyes of our commander. "Excuse me, sir."

"—and showing her that insignia on its unitard, the one Ernie told us about from inside the facility."

A thoughtful grunt emitted from Sarge.

Dahlia looked at the insignia and remembered what Ernie had said as well. She said gently but with enough projection that the dying alien could hear her, "What does this mean? Tell me and we can get you some help." A lie, but one that could not only help us but also perhaps give the mortally wounded bastard a little hope.

"Hhhhelllllp? Hhhhhow …?"

"We're getting into that underground facility—there are three doctors there. They can try to help you."

At that, the bugger's eyes grew wide with fear. "Nnnnnohhh, nefferrrr go thhhhere! Neffffffer! Pllllllleassse dhhhonnn't

taaakhhhe mee dhowwwwn aghaaaainnn! I w-wonnnn't bhee a
wwwarrr dhaaaagh ..."

"What? Why not? Why shouldn't we go down there? What's a
war dog? Please tell me!"

It trembled as he spoke, and Dahlia didn't think this was from
being cold and near death: "Rrrhipplle ... Ghhhorrrellmannn ...
B-Bissssssshahhp ... theyyy mmmakhe ... *mahnnnsterrrrs ...*"

After it struggled to breathe out those final words—the names
of the three whitecoats we were supposed to be rescuing and then
that last word, which was definitely *monsters*—the Yellow grew
very still, and then his body relaxed to the point of seeming
deflated. It was dead.

Dahlia did a few quick checks for what, on a human at least,
would be his vital signs. Finding none, she looked at us and shook
her head.

Sarge made the motion for her to return to us, which she stood
and did immediately.

"Sir, the Xeno knew I was a Space Navy grunt. It said the word.
I guess by my uniform, it identified me as infantry. It knows the
names of the whitecoats downstairs. It said they make *monsters*."

Sarge nodded to let her know the information has seeped into
his noggin. Then he asked, "Did it happen to mention how we get
through this goddamn doors?"

"It didn't, sir. And I don't think it would have—it was adamant
that we *not* go down there."

"Understood. I respectfully disregard his advice."

"I hoped you would, sir," Dahlia said. "That thing may know
some Terran Standard, but it doesn't grok *loyalty* or *mission*.
These Xenos are animals, I don't care how human they try to look
or imitate our speech."

"That's my girl," Sarge said and turned to Killshot: "We've lost time—let's get to that devil's nutsack of a gazebo and erase it from Planet Bunghole."

"Aye, sir!" the three grunts left tried to cheer in unison, but exhaustion was in our voices and starting to creep into our minds. Nevertheless, we followed Sarge's lead in double-timing it to the drop site and one last try at rescuing our very-possibly-alive platoon mates and the whitecoats we were sent here to extract.

But for all that, the dying Yellow's warning advice not to do this imbued every step with a darkling sense of dread that made me want to go anywhere but that underground house of horrors.

As usual, Sarge knew his troops and could read my mind like he had a psychic Enhancement: "Men, we have a mission to fulfill. I don't know what's down in that lab, but whatever it is, we are goddamn Space Navy SEALs and we do our duty. *Capische?*"

"Sir! Capische, sir!"

That made him bark out a laugh. "Well done, assholes. Now let's do some damage."

***

On our march toward doom—if not at the hands of the Grays, then definitely by execution for the mutiny of killing aliens we were for some reason specifically ordered *not* to kill—we grew serious again and focused on the task at hand: that gazebo was going to be matchsticks and we were getting downstairs, case closed.

We exited the path that, now that we noticed, was well trod indeed, with small, medium, and large footprints (I assume for human, yellow, and gray.) And there they were: the space elevator cable stretching into invisibility, and not fifty yards from that, the *Music Man* gazebo ready for a 1900-era barbershop quartet. (These references almost make me laugh—if it weren't for my perfect recall of everything I've ever seen, *I* would have no idea what I was talking about.)

We didn't stop—we didn't even slow down. In fact, Sarge picked up speed, the unbreakable Dahlia accelerating right next to him. Killshot and I held back, scrawny for SEALs compared to those two. No weapons drawn, no special Space/Earth tactics, just our massive commander and hard-as-an-iron-core remaining infantryman running full bore at the wooden structure, war ululations released in the seconds before impact.

And impact they did. The glass panels with the Science Division logo on them instantly exploded into dime-sized fragments; the wooden supports snapped, bringing down the canopy and roof. But those hadn't fallen to the ground before Sarge and Dahlia barreled through to the other side, destroying those supports as well and leveled the whole damned thing.

"Step One complete," Killshot said to me with a smirk. "And I didn't feel a thing."

I grinned at that, and we moved a little faster to get to the pile of sticks and splinters that was all there was left of the above-the-floor structure of the gazebo. Sarge and Dahlia caught their breath for maybe thirty seconds before stepping up to help remove the debris from our real target: that mother-lovin' trapdoor.

There were still the two steps leading up to the floor of the gazebo, and of course the floor itself, both needing to be demolished if the trapdoor didn't come quietly. "Killshot, wriggle yourself between the stairs and the wall there, see what we got under there."

"Aye, sir," our sniper said, and used his snakelike slimness and enhanced eyesight to get under our feet as we stared at the shut door. He then yelled—our comms were out, so he was making sure we could all hear him—"We got an anthill, Sarge. None of the base of the gazebo is made of supports. It's hollow down here."

"Excellent. Come on out."

The trapdoor being "an anthill" mean that it was a vertical shaft coming up out of the ground to meet the wooden floor of the gazebo. In other words, as Killshot had described it, the lower part of the gazebo was "hollow"—it wasn't supporting the shaft and the shaft wasn't supporting the structure. This means it would be much easier to take down everything but the anthill topped by the trapdoor, and then we could try to break in the side of the shaft or just vaporize it with our plasma weapons. That hadn't worked on the trapdoor itself, however.

Plain wood from the Terra-like trees was a different story. "I'll take north," Sarge said, and proceeded to point to each of us and then our cardinal direction: "Boswell, northeast; Dahlia, southeast; Killshot, right next to me."

We each took our positions. It was obvious what Sarge was going to have us do, as we had talked about it all during the mission as soon as we found out we had brought toys to a tank fight—we'd concentrate our weapons on one spot for maximum damage, although it wouldn't compare to the power of one railgun shot.

"On my mark, people: One, two, th—"

The trapdoor slid open.

Nothing came out. A quick look around showed nothing was trying to get in.

Sarge shook his head and let out a single chuckle: "Heh."

Mesmerized by the precise timing of the open door, it took a moment for the rest of us to focus on Sarge. "Sir?" Dahlia said.

"You finally get a plan that'll work, and then the damned thing doesn't even let you use it. Infantry, check the hole."

Dahlia crab-walked to the gazebo steps and across the wooden floor. She looked down into the hole. "Nothing to report, sir. Just the vertical shaft with the handholds, as before."

"Door's not trying to slide back?"

"No, sir."

Sarge chewed his lip for a moment, then said, "Boswell? Speculate, please."

"Sir, we're being invited in. I don't know if that's good or bad," I said. "It's good, since we were about to try to blast our way in anyway; but bad, because obviously, whatever is down there knows we're here. Any element of surprise we might have possessed is gone."

"There never was an element of surprise," Sarge said, giving the treeline a perfunctory scan. "They've been watching us this whole time."

Killshot almost choked in protest. "Sarge, I *always* keep an eye out for vidcams, robotic optics, drones—everything!"

"Easy, soldier. I know you do."

"Then ... how could they be watching us, sir?"

"My guess is it ain't vidcams or robotic optics or drones. They could have cams in the eyes of the mammalogues. Maybe there's a photon sink in each blade of this grass. It don't matter. But they've definitely been watching."

"Who has, Sarge?"

"Let's find out," he said after another frustrated glance around. "Dahlia, you're first down the hole. Then Killshot, me, and Boswell bringing up the rear. Understood? Then *go*, people!"

For a woman as solid as she was, Dahlia was disarmingly light on her feet. She just hopped up and into the hole and caught the top rung with her fingers and a lower rung with her feet, so she was able to fluidly and immediately start down the shaft. Killshot went in more traditionally, since a sprain or broken finger on his body wouldn't fix itself; he put one leg down, then another, and walked down the rungs until he could employ his hands and descend faster.

Sarge went next, and I seriously thought his bulk wouldn't fit through the hole in the floor. But he had been doing all this for a long time, and he got one massive leg in, then eased the other, then walked down a few rungs as Killshot had done, and finally slipped down one arm, his head, and then the other arm, each limb of his body just making it through the opening. Then I took one last quick look around to make sure we weren't being followed, and got myself down the shaft as well.

No sooner had my head cleared the opening than the trapdoor slid shut.

Sarge heard and then saw it happen. He grunted a laugh and said, "This is good practice for when we have to climb down to Hell."

***

The vertical shaft was slightly skewed—this was why we couldn't see what was at the other end of the tunnel. But after only two dozen feet or so, the shaft ended and we each climbed down to the last rung with our hands and then dropped the ten feet to the floor of a very ordinary and clean-looking laboratory facility hallway. A floor-maintenance robot hummed past us.

"That explains why it doesn't look like any mud-footed aliens have been through here lately," Killshot said. "The walls aren't damaged, either, though. Not too much of a struggle with the whitecoats, I guess."

Sarge acknowledged our sniper's comments with a grunt. Then he cocked his head like he heard something to our left and said, "This way."

We took out our plasma weapons, which could at least have given someone or something pause before it could kill us like the scientists. Or had one gone mad down here and killed the other two? That wouldn't have been the first time it happened. The doors and such *did* seem guided by a creature more delicately sentient than the Yellows or Grays, however, so I couldn't guess how a single whitecoat kept them all at bay. Maybe there were interior barriers? I couldn't correlate everything I knew—for every explanation, there was a counterexample. For every assumption one made, there was some fact or other assumption that plainly violated it. With me, of course, there was no question that I had *forgotten* any element of the situation, but it was the fitting together of the disparate parts that eluded me completely. Maybe that was why I was merely a logman and not a tactician.

Pistols drawn, two of us clung to either wall as we made our way around a long curve, making our way as stealthily as possible. We watched for shadows, listened for footsteps, made ourselves alert to any change in the situ—

"Welcome, soldiers," a thin, small woman in a white lab coat said warmly. She stood directly in the middle of the curving corridor, and we didn't see her until we were upon her.

Everyone, including Sarge, gave a start, but fortunately our plasma weapons had to be charged for an instant before they could be fired. No one shot, and now no one moved. But every pistol was pointed directly at the woman's face, which showed no tension whatsoever. I recognized her face from the picture Ernie had given us after he picked up her radio message. And I wasn't the only one.

"Doctor Ripple," Sarge said. "You know who we are." Neither sentence was a question?

"Yes, Chief *War Thug*," she replied with a small smile, "you are the remainder of the crew of Space Navy vessel the *Blue Celeste*. We're the ones who called for help, you'll remember."

"We're here to extract you and your two colleagues. Um … Boswell, *names*."

"Lieutenant Doctor Andy Bishop and Second Lieutenant Michael Gorelman, sir."

To me: "Thank you." To Ripple: "Where are they right now?"

Ripple indicated somewhere down her end of the hall. "They're in the containment lab."

"Mm-hmm. And where are the other members of our platoon, Doctor?"

"They are also in the containment lab." She turned to her right and motioned that we were welcome to go farther into the facility. Getting a nod from Sarge, she took the lead. "Before you ask— yes, they are all alive and well. In fact, we've all been waiting for you to make your appearance down here."

"We have a lot of questions for you, Doctor," Sarge said as we followed the woman through the hall, where doors finally appeared. They were windowless and unmarked. Other than keeping our weapons drawn, we took no action to protect ourselves from anything that might be hiding behind those doors. There were just too many threats, even though the facility appeared as if there was no danger at all. "What are those yellow and gray Xenofauna? Why are they dressed in uniforms with insignia—?"

"We have a long trip back to the base, don't we? There will be plenty of time for questions and answers."

"It's not that long of a trip in subspace, Doctor. And I have a *lot* of questions."

"Of course you do." Ripple arrived at a door that looked exactly the same as the twenty or so we had already passed. This one, however, had a huge palm pad against which Ripple placed her hand to be allowed entry. It was lost on none of us that even one of the gray aliens could splay its entire palm against the surface of that pad.

Now that I took a good look at the ceilings, they weren't ten feet high. I counted off each unit in my head as I took a mental measurement.

They were *eleven* feet high. Something ten feet tall could easily walk inside this facility. I had no idea what that could mean. Did the scientists or the War Council already know the height of half of Planet Bunghole's indigenous, semi-sentient population? Were the yellow Xenos taught to speak here?

Come to think of it, what the hell was being *contained* inside that room?

At her touch on the pad, the door slid open, and we saw for ourselves.

***

What was contained in there was Leonard, Junebug, Inman, Hog, Gunner, Fugly, Ernie, and Calico. Each of them stood alone in a cell with a transparent barrier in front and yellow walls inside. The cells were positioned in a line, making up one wall of the large room, and so none of my platoon-mates could see any other.

They saw us, though, and started beating on the transparent wall to get our attention. They looked to be yelling or even screaming, but not one vibration made it to our ears.

Enraged, our commander leveled his plasma weapon at Ripple's mousy-brown-haired head. "Talk now or never talk again, *Doctor*."

Dahlia, Killshot, and I exchanged a glance. We had no idea what to do, so each of us also aimed our weapon at the transcendently calm whitecoat.

Ripple said, "Of course I will talk to you, War Thug. The guns aren't necessary."

"They ain't guns. They're plasma pistols. And sorry to disagree, but I *do* find them necessary right now."

"Go ahead," she said. "Open fire. Any of you, all of you. Reduce me to cinders."

I couldn't see Sarge's face, but I knew he must have been narrowing his eyes in suspicion. "Sniper, discharge your weapon at that fire-suppression sprinkler head in the wall. Get all this *research equipment* nice and soaked."

"Aye, sir," Killshot said, and thumbed the switch to charge and squeezed the trigger to unleash the plasma bolt and melt the metal target into … "Ah, Sarge, nothing's happening."

"Dahlia, give it a try," Sarge said, but he already sounded resigned.

She did. "Nothing, sir."

Doctor Ripple smiled and said, "This room is dampened to affect all weapons, from plasma pistols to railguns. Too dangerous in this environment, you must realize. I don't know why you would want to blast my head off anyway, War Thug. Your soldiers are unharmed and absolutely safe—"

"I don't care if I *blast* it off. How about I just *rip* it off?" Sarge took a step toward her, and an enormous gray arm came out of nowhere and looped itself around Sarge's head, its muscles dwarfing our commander's. The Gray stepped out from the shadows—none of us had even noticed that side of the room existed, so focused were we on our mates trapped on the other side—and immobilized Sarge's arms by wrapping its tree-trunk arms around his torso.

Sarge didn't struggle. He wasn't being choked; he wasn't being crushed. For the moment, at least, he was just being *neutralized.*

Dahlia moved to charge Ripple, but Sarge barked for her to keep her position. She did so immediately without complaint. Without *verbal* complaint, anyway.

"War Thug, you and your troops are here to *rescue* us," a baritone voice spoke from the shadows that had previously hidden the giant alien. A tall, handsome man stepped out to stand beside Ripple. "Why are you threatening to *kill* us?"

"Doctor Bishop," Killshot said. This was another familiar face, easy to recognize. "What in the hell is going on here, sir? Why are our men in cages? And these Xenos—have you enslaved the alien population, against War Council protocol to exterminate them?"

"Ellen was right—so many questions!" Bishop said with a laugh. "Don't worry. All will be made clear very shortly. It must be obvious that any attack, Enhanced or not, will fail, so please just take your fellow Council service members at our word that everyone is unharmed?"

"I have an eidetic memory Enhancement," I said without prompting, "and I've seen enough vidfilms to recognize that you and Doctor Ripple are acting transparently *eeevil* in the way villains are portrayed in the worst melodramas. As I am the commander's second, I demand that you tell us what is going on here, why you two are acting so oddly, and where Lieutenant Gorelman is at this moment."

"Demand?" Bishop gawked at me, then at Sarge, then at Ripple, all the time with a smile turning up the corners of his surprise-opened mouth. Then he said to me, "These vidfilms, you're talking about espionage and action-adventure narratives, correct?"

"Ay—er, *correct*." This man had not earned an *aye* from me.

"I have seen these vidfilms. The *villains*, as you call them, are often trying to forge a new world, or at least put themselves at the top of it. Idealists, really."

Oh, hell, I thought, *so they're embracing the dark side.*

"But those megalomaniacs will kill indiscriminately to reach their goal, which is most often tied to personal wealth and power. As members of the War Council's Science Division, we work to *save* lives. We're using Enhancement technology to create *super-soldiers* who are as superior to our current Enhanced fighters as the members of your platoon are to the soldiers in the time before Enhancement technology was created. These super-soldiers will each eliminate more alien terrorist threats than an entire platoon of current SEALs. They will be Earth's key to victory."

Okay, maybe they *weren't* on the dark side of this situation. The plan didn't sound *eeevil*, or even evil, just a natural step forward in the permanent War Against Alien Aggression. Platoons like ours were the super-soldiers of the past fifty years, outfitted with better and better Enhancements to more effectively wipe out our enemies and seize their technology for study. So it made sense that the War Council was trying to Enhance its fighting forces even more. "All right," I said at last, "maybe you aren't villains. But then why have you taken our platoon-mates hostage and imprisoned them in solitary confinement? And I insist on asking again: Where is Lieutenant Gorelman?"

"He's right here," Doctor Ripple said with a mocking smile. "Who do you think is presently keeping your War Thug from doing anything stupid?"

Our eyes immediately shifted from Ripple's face to that of the Gray holding Sarge immobile. We had all seen Gorelman's image on our HUD, but my memory was the sharpest, of course. And I saw that the human-like face of the hulking monster was indeed that of Second Lieutenant Michael Gorelman.

So it wasn't a human-*like* face. It was a *human* face.

And that meant the rest of the giant gray monster was Gorelman as well. The ten-foot-tall creatures weren't Xenos at all—this *thing* was an Enhancement of the Science Department lieutenant. This was a human being, a Terran.

"What did you *do* to him?" Dahlia said as soon as she could process what she was seeing and just heard.

"Nothing he didn't want to be done," Ripple said. "He came here with Doctor Bishop and myself specifically to test whether GHE—that's Global Human Enhancement—was possible." She looked with pride at the now-enormous Gorelman, who was grinning at their achievement.

"It wasn't just possible—it was amazingly straightforward!" Bishop gushed, apparently not seeing or not caring about our horrified expressions. "The right frequency of radiation on the glandular system starts the multiplying muscle cells, but it takes time, so much time. Michael showed us that GHE candidates go through a yellow phase once the growth chemicals are begun in conjunction with the radiation Enhancement therapy. We didn't see that happening at all."

"We all went through the radiation therapy on our glands, *Herr Doktor*," Killshot said. "The frequency allows malleability of Enhancement, but the body of the subject has to *accept* it. My Enhanced vision fit with my genotype and phenotype; Sarge's Enhanced muscles wouldn't have worked—"

"I don't have muscle Enhancements, soldier." Sarge was calm, still held in place by the former Michael Gorelman. "Not that kind, anyway. I juice with Betelgeuse Mammalogue Extract, and then lift heavy things like your stupid ass in battle."

This made our sniper smile. "Okay, Sarge. Then what is your Enhancement?"

"Classified," Sarge said, "but you knew that."

"I thought a special moment like this might be the icebreaker I've been looking for to get you to tell all." Killshot laughed, which was what he did when he was nervous. Or not nervous. Sarge put up with it because it relieved tension, but all the tension relief in the world wasn't going to get our compatriots out of those cages, so he gave Killshot the signal for *Secure the chatter*.

"We won't have any trouble finding out what those are, Chief," Ripple said. "Once you receive the initial doses of radiation at the correct frequency, your Enhancements … how should I say this … will *express themselves* in wholly unpredictable ways. If you have Enhancements that agree with our technique, you will grow into the magnificent form that Michael has taken on here. What was your original Enhancement, Lieutenant?"

The human face on what now was obviously a hugely perverted human body looked stricken. Gorelman opened his mouth and let out something between a squeak and a grunt. (Prior to this, we had only heard the Grays roar.)

"Oh, that's right! Sorry, Michael, didn't mean to put you on the spot." She then addressed us again: "The one drawback to making these super-soldiers is that their anatomy no longer allows for speech. But our big boys here are meant to receive orders and execute those orders. They don't have anything to say that the Council wants to hear, anyway—they'll be accompanied by Enhanced soldiers like you lot for when communication with command is necessary."

Dahlia thought of this first, but it was creeping in the back of my mind as well: "Doctor Ripple … what happens if a soldier's Enhancements *don't* agree with your, um, *technique*?"

The small woman laughed. "I'm sorry, I didn't mean to make it sound so *sinister*. The radiation on the proper areas of the glandular system will make huge and positive changes to any subject. Those whose *Enhancements* don't work with the technique still become seven-foot-tall, explosively muscled soldiers, better at fighting and killing than any of you, if, unfortunately, not as good at thinking or speaking."

None of us had to say it out loud. These were the Yellows, hunted by the Grays.

"We saw your bigger mutants hunting and killing the smaller ones. And we heard a yellow one speak. Its dying words were spent telling us not to come down here."

Bishop chuckled. "Dying, huh?" He addressed the Gorelman-thing: "You guys are being careless. We need clean, fast kills in the field, Lieutenant. Get that through your men's thickened skulls ASAP."

Gorelman nodded, looking miserable. I wondered how a non-speaking creature could give a pep talk to a bunch of similar mutes. Maybe they had worked out some kind of sign language to communicate using their enormous hands and fingers.

"And speaking of deaths in the field … War Thug, you killed three of our very valuable super-soldiers with your bare hands. Ninety percent of what we create here become the smaller, yellow forces. Only ten percent make it to the top and become our ten-foot heroes. And you killed *three* of these precious commodities."

"Wish I'd gotten more, asshat."

Bishop and Ripple nodded and smirked at each other. Ripple said, "Now *that's* the War Thug we've been waiting to see! Maybe intense aggression is your Enhancement, something that comes out only in a fight. We've read your dossier from the Council—you love to kill, *live* to kill anything threatening Earth or even seeming like it could evolve to threaten our home. Very admirable. You will be one of our gray corps when you finish therapy, I think."

"Agreed," Bishop said. "That automail forearm of yours is not technically an Enhancement, correct?"

Sarge shrugged, looking at us like *Why not tell them? Who gives a rat's ass what they know?* Dahlia and Killshot and I could hardly have agreed more. "I lost the lower half of my arm to a goddamned *bug* because I got careless during a goddamned simple bug hunt. Maybe they could've reattached it, but I grabbed it out of the bug's mouth with my left hand and beat that alien piece of garbage to death with it. Unfortunately, using the arm as a weapon created too much vascular damage for it to be reattached. Which is fine—I friggin' *love* my metal arm."

Bishop waited. "And so …?"

"So it's *not* an Enhancement like what SEALs get to help them hunt and kill more efficiently, all right, jerkoff? But the way my muscles have grown around its base to accept it—that might be something. I don't really remember myself what they did to me after I enlisted. Except make me *even more friggin' AWESOME*."

"Well, huzzah, tough guy—we're going to make you *ten times* as awesome. In the containment areas—what you lot keep referring to as *cages*—we have already begun the initial radiation frequency therapy on your comrades in arms."

For the first time, Sarge made a strong move to get out from Gorelman's hold. "You sons of bitches are experimenting on *my men?* I will break your lousy necks—"

"We're not *experimenting*," Ripple said with her evil-calm voice. "The concept has been proven and is Council-approved. What we're doing now is *implementation*."

My platoon-mates saw us looking over at them again, and again they banged on the transparent wall. Killshot narrowed his eyes at them and said quietly to me, "They're screaming for us to *run*, to *get away before it's too late*."

"Sounds like good advice," I whispered, "once we get them out of there."

Killshot smiled at me. We were a team, a *platoon*.

Ripple continued: "War Thug, you will be first into the containment area, where we will dispense with the initial low-frequency diagnosis phase and go right into making you a big gray order-follower like the Lieutenant here. The rest of your unit will see that it's much better—we can kill far more terrorist aliens with men like him, and like you once we get you up to size."

Dahlia spoke up, wanting to delay this as long as possible while we wracked our brains for a violent solution. "Why do you let the Grays kill the Yellows? Aren't you wasting resources? And who are these people you've turned into monsters, anyway? Slave-planet prisoners? Condemned War Council traitors?"

"No, dear girl!" Ripple said in surprise. "We can't have sleaze turned into anything but more powerful sleaze. No, all of our super-soldiers, bigger and smaller, were originally sent to us as law-abiding humans by the War Council. Only those whose bodies accepted Enhancement are right for this next step in fighting technology."

My blood went cold. "*Enhanced* humans?" As far as I remembered—which was everything—only select military forces received Enhancement. "Who?"

"I can see on your face that you just got it. The Council sends us you guys, Space Navy SEALs! The best and brightest, most vicious and ruthless fighters in the galaxy! They send platoon after platoon on a mission to 'extract scientists in danger.' We test your problem-solving and fighting ability aboveground—good job, by the way, troops—and see if you are promising candidates for further, *super-soldier* Enhancements."

I wanted to puke, and I hadn't puked since basic training on Mars. Dahlia and Killshot carried the same expressions of nausea and anger I felt on my own face.

Dahlia repeated, "Why do you allow the Grays to hunt and kill the Yellows? You'd better not make me a super-soldier, because I will separate your head from your body the second I'm out of that cage." Her lips quivered with rage. "Also, I hope you go blind and your children get instant-metastasis Stage Four cancer."

"All right, soldier, enough of that," Bishop said, dismissively waving her words away. "Once you are irradiated to Stage 1— what you call a 'Yellow'—your anti-Council treachery is pardoned. Yes, we know all about your mutinous conversations— and of course your boss here murdered three of our super-soldiers against the strictest orders not to, so he would be doomed anyway without this pardon. When you have gone through the whole two weeks of radiation frequency and genetic therapy, you won't even remember your traitorous acts. You will forget everything but being willing to kill and die at any whim of the War Council. You may remember a *few* things—your talkative yellow friend who warned you not to come here must have not have had his memory fully wiped through our process. But you will be one step closer to being a true super-soldier. Even if we can't Enhance you further, and you remain a Yellow, you will still be an insanely powerful fighter and presence on the battlefield."

"So answer my goddamn question: *Why do you let the Grays kill the Yellows?*"

"We don't *let* them do it, soldier," Ripple said. "We *make* them do it. It's part of their training as super-soldiers, for the actual gray supers to hunt the lesser heroes and kill as many of them as possible. We release the Yellows into the environment, see how well they can survive. Wherever they are on the planet—and we have a portal tunnel none of you have clearance to even hear details about—the Yellows must get back to our gazebo to be *safe*. This way the Grays get hunting practice with big game, and we weed out the Yellows who aren't fast or clever or lucky enough to elude the bigger soldiers. The ones who *are* able to survive are sent into battle on planets where we don't have enough soldiers to subdue any threats. These Yellows are the very best of Stage 1. Most of them stay here for hunting by 'the Grays.' We have seeded them all over L-22233."

Sarge kept his game face, but it looked pale as he said, "So you have SEALs, the most effective and dedicated fighting force in history, hunting and killing *other SEALs?* This whole planet is populated by deformed mutants created from *those sworn to serve the Council?* You pieces of—"

"Now, now, Chief, let's not get all high and mighty on this. We have enough vidcam footage of you and your platoon complaining about the War Council for you all to be executed immediately upon your return to base. So you can work with us, or you can go back with your mission of extracting us unfulfilled—and you know how much the Council *hates* that—*and* with evidence we provide of your anti-Council plotting."

Sarge said no more, but fumed like hell. For his own sake, Gorelman would be wise not to let his arms relax, even for a moment.

"It's a devil's choice, I know, but all of you will become either Yellows or Grays. It is the ultimate fighting force, yes, but also it is each of your *fulfilling your oath to protect Earth.* Individuals, even platoons, don't matter. What matters is that we win the fight against alien aggression."

Ripple added, "I do believe your commander here will be a massive and powerful Gray," Bishop said, looking admiringly at Sarge. "And I didn't even tell you the best part, War Thug."

"Oh, yeah?"

"The Yellows that the Grays hunt and kill? They're members of the Grays' *own former platoon.* Once you're a Stage 2, you'll forget all about who they were to you and just see 'aliens' to kill. If there are five who survive the additional month of radiation and therapy and become Grays, those five Grays will hunt the 45 smaller supers—your Yellows.

"But none of this would be launching yet if I didn't get *you,* War Thug. You are a murderous bastard in the name of the War Council, our biggest in-the-field achiever! Just think what you will do once you're ten feet tall and receptive to any order we make." Ripple was enjoying the hell out of this. "We have this planet almost fully stocked with super-Enhanced soldiers, ready to put them to work wiping out all non-human life in this quadrant of the galaxy, all to protect the homeland."

"Planet Bunghole," Killshot said. "Tastes as great as its name."

Ripple didn't understand our nickname for the planet, which amused us even more than if she had. "You're our *sine qua non*, War Thug. Once you and your platoon have gone through the process, we will *extract*, as we say, every super-soldier on the planet. It's time to win this war."

Bishop nodded and said, "Okay, that's enough talk—Michael, put War Thug in the central containment area so all of his comrades can watch him *improve* right before their eyes."

The Gorelman-thing turned Sarge toward the transparent cylinder in the center of the room, and to my surprise, Sarge didn't fight it. However, when they were right outside the *special containment unit*, he addressed the whitecoats: "I will do this willingly if you let the rest of my platoon return to the *Blue Celeste* without being ... what the hell was it? ... *super-Enhanced*."

Ripple looked at Bishop, who gave a small shrug and said, "I believe that's fair, considering he could probably kill us all after the first few treatments."

"I could kill you all right now," Sarge said calmly.

"But we don't *need* you to do anything willingly, War Thug. Fight all you want."

"Wait a minute," I said. "What happens after the first few treatments?"

"With your commander's particular Enhancement, it's hard to tell exactly what will happen. It's very exciting."

It felt like a betrayal to ask, but I said to Bishop, "So what *is* his Enhancement?"

"I oughta kick your ass, Boswell."

I tried not to freak out over crossing the line. "I'm sorry, sir, but it's a *need-to-know* question if we are to rescue you."

Ripple laughed. *"Rescue* him? What, one logman with no Enhanced-fighting abilities, a sniper without a rifle or long-range target, and an infantryman who can, what, *heal herself* until we surrender?" She laughed again, this time more in astonishment than bemusement like most of what tickled her funny bone. "Master Chief Petty Officer ———— is Enhanced with *targeted rage*, like a shark in a feeding frenzy. Surely you have seen him in this mode? Almost fatherly and protective of his men, but pure terror to anything Xenotypic, completely without mercy.

"Our hope is that he will become an indiscriminate agent of rage and chaos on any alien world we drop him onto. But don't worry, he'll be well trained on how to hunt using his heightened Stage 2 Enhancements. I don't plan to continue any radiation and gene therapy of you grunts beyond Stage 1. You'll grow in height to seven feet and gain strength far beyond that of even a strength-Enhanced normal human. Your skin will turn waxy yellow as it becomes malleable enough to accommodate your new physique.

"But your *Sarge* here will join with the other gray, ten-foot-tall Stage 2 super-soldiers. His murderous training will be considered finished once he has brought to the lab the head of every one of his former platoon-mates. *Bring me the head of my enemy*, kind of old-timey stuff, you know? Just like our gazebo—it makes a statement."

"I'll make a statement—you are a couple of goddamned lunatics," Killshot said.

"Oh my god, I forgot you were there, soldier! And you and you," Ripple said as she pointed to each of us in turn. "We would like you all to take a seat inside one of the open containment compartments."

"You mean *cages*," Dahlia said. "You're holding Space/Earth Atmosphere Leapers, the best troops in the whole Space Navy, inside cages like we're DNA-reconstituted rhinos at the zoo!" She leapt at Ripple but, again, out of the shadows stepped another tremendous Gray alien—only it wasn't an alien at all, but a Space Navy SEAL—and grabbed Dahlia's arm and held her in place.

"We're SEALs!" our infantryman shouted at the Gray's human face. "We're your comrades!"

"Let her go, Biehn." The super-soldier unwrapped his fingers from Dahlia's arm and stepped back into the shadows. "They don't remember anything about who or what they used to be. All they know now is following orders, which they do *perfectly*," Ripple said, smiling at her creation. "For example, recall when one of our Stage 1 super-soldiers grabbed your platoon-mate and threatened to kill him if the pack of Stage 2 soldiers didn't cease their hunting him that day?"

"Yeah," Killshot said. "The Grays backed off like the Yellow was a nuke on a hair trigger."

"They were under orders not to kill any humans—at least those who hadn't begun their therapy yet. And they didn't. Quite unlike what you did with the Council's order that no *aliens* be killed on L-22233, isn't that right, Chief?"

Sarge didn't bother looking at her as he said, "We thought they were killing our people, possibly even eating them. I followed a course of action that I believed would lessen their numbers, give us a chance to get into this facility, rescue our men, and liberate you asshole whitecoats."

"Irradiating and training Stage 2 super-soldiers is *very* expensive! You disobeyed a direct order from *the War Council itself!*"

"I do that sometimes," Sarge said, although I had never seen him do it.

"Well, you'll never have to worry about doing it again," she said, and slid a small slider on a control panel, causing the two-walled cylinder to turn until an opening was visible. "Once you get to Stage 2, your memories are gone, your former identity has been wiped away, and your only purpose in the universe is to follow War Council directives *to the letter*. You'll be unable *not* to."

The Gorelman-thing was about to shove Sarge into the cylinder when Ripple yelled, "*Wait!*"

The Gray waited.

Bishop laughed and grabbed a mean-looking hook device. "Holy crap, that would not have gone well," he said to Bishop. "Getting sloppy in my old age."

I couldn't tell what the tool was, but it looked *very* powerful and *very* likely to grab onto something and never let go. "What the hell are you doing?" I said, knowing that whether they told me or not, I was about to see with my own eyes what they were about to do.

Ripple sauntered to Bishop's side, and if Sarge hadn't been well and truly held in place by the thing that used to be Lieutenant Michael Gorelman, he would have torn both of the scientists in half with his bare hands. Ripple said to Dahlia, Killshot, and me, "This is a device that causes *serious* pain, even for one as juiced up and stoic as your commander here. Doctor Bishop will not hesitate to dig right in if you and your two compatriots don't get your asses into those containment pods immediately. Double-time. *Go.*"

What else could we do? We marched our way to the three open containers and each of us entered and sat on the bunk built into the wall. The transparent, apparently indestructible, door slid shut, and now all I could see was Sarge, Gorelman, and the two whitecoats. I couldn't hear anything at all, and I knew from my platoon-mates' silent screams that no one would be able to hear me, either.

That was probably good, because I started screaming in protest at the top of my lungs and pounding with all of my strength on the door as Ripple took a scalpel and ran it down the length of Sarge's right forearm. There was a little blood toward the top, but no such gore as the scalpel glided down to his hand.

She then put her fingers into the incision and pulled the flesh back.

Sarge had a prosthetic arm, just like Leonard did. Automail, fully functional, the works.

Before I could finish admiring the workmanship, however, Bishop fired up the claw-tool and let 'er rip on Sarge's right arm, just below the elbow.

I actually gasped. *They were separating his mechanical arm from his body.* To do that, they would have to rip through every tendon and nerve that had insinuated itself around and inside the carbon-nanotube construction. And that's just what they did. As the machine did its work, blood and sinew flew everywhere and before the task was completed, I could see that Sarge was screaming, tears of agony rolling down his cheeks.

When it was done, they cauterized the stump with plasma beams, hot like the ones in our sidearms. Sarge looked like he could barely even scream anymore.

Ripple, that bitch, tapped a metal circle on her white coat's collar and said, "Sorry you had to see that, troopers. We can't have a lot of metal in the therapy booth—the radiation makes metal so hot it can kill anyone it's attached to. And we wouldn't want anything to happen to ol' War Thug here, would we?" She tapped the circle again and I was once again in silence.

Sarge looked like they had taken the fight out of him with imprisoning the soldiers he took an oath to protect. They had ripped off an arm that was much more than a prosthetic, seeing that it was connected to his nervous system and musculature. Now he was stripped naked and forced into god knew what fate, but definitely one that would erase the sentient fighting man and replace him with an unquestioning, uncaring, solitary killing machine barely distinguishable from an actual terrorist alien.

He was pushed into the cylinder by Gorelman the Gray, and the walls quickly slid around to eliminate the opening. Sarge didn't move, bang on the transparent material, nothing. He just stared at his discarded, blood-and-tissue–splattered automail arm. For a moment, he got that sardonic smile on his face, then shook it away and stared at the eleven of us in our cages. Finally, he looked down at his feet, probably seeing nothing at all.

Now Bishop and Ripple darted around the various control panels, pushing buttons and sliders, flipping switches. The Gorelman-thing just stood silently at attention, waiting for his next order. Finally, the two whitecoats stepped into a small room with protective glass and put on protective eyewear. I couldn't hear what order was given to Gorelman, but the Gray slipped back into the shadows like the other a moment earlier.

Ripple smiled at Bishop and opened a plastic clamshell protecting a large green button from being pressed accidentally. Then she slapped her palm against the button and—

—and we were plunged into darkness. An instant later, we could see Sarge writhing in pain as the green light of whatever frequency radiation they were using flooded the room. An agonizing sixty seconds later, the green light vanished and the facility's lighting returned to normal.

My hands were against the cell door as I tried to see what had happened to our commander. I'm sure everyone else's were, too.

But the only people capable of seeing what effect the initial radiation treatment had on Sarge were Ripple and Bishop, who stripped off their safety eyewear and rushed to push the slider that opened the cylinder. Sarge was curled in a ball on the floor of the cylinder, even after the opening was once again created.

As they approached our commander, the two Grays stepped back into the light and followed them. Ripple pressed the microphone on her coat again and spoke to us grunts. "Your Chief will be all right, soldiers. Everyone reacts a little differently to the initial dose of frequency radiation. Some are frightened and try to protect themselves the way animals do. That looks like what War Thug is doing. But others have a more ... *active* reaction. That's why these two super-soldiers are on standby while we check— *gerrrrk—*"

That last sound was Doctor Ripple's own fascinating reaction to Sarge shoving his giant Gray hand through her chest, tearing through her lungs, her heart, anything in its path and shoving those parts out her back onto the tile floor.

Sarge's skin had turned as gray as the Grays' now. And, as he unfolded himself from the cylinder, he stood over the two super-soldiers, at least two feet taller than the monsters in the lab. Bishop yelled something and pointed at Sarge (as if the pair couldn't see him). His order must have been to subdue Sarge, because as ill-advised as it seemed, Gorelman and his unfortunate partner made a beeline toward War Thug, who was smashing every computer and every bit of technology he could reach with his remaining hand and his stump. He kicked the cylinder he had formerly been trapped in and it *shattered*. Transparent aluminium had never been known to shatter. (Well, now it had.)

The Grays coming right at him, Sarge made a juke move like someone playing Rollerball and got around them both. It took the twelve-foot enraged monster two steps to reach Bishop, who looked like he was soiling himself in terror. Sarge reached down and lifted the scientist by his legs, turning him upside-down. By the time the two stooge Grays arrived, our commander was able to swing Bishop like a baseball bat against Gorelman, making the normal-sized human's head explode in gore and his body almost liquify at the force of Sarge's swing.

Gorelman was knocked into the other Gray—the other once-brave and loyal Space Navy SEAL—and they tripped over each other. As they fell to the floor, Sarge snapped Gorelman's neck with his left hand and caved in the face and skull of his partner, leaving them both unmoving heaps.

Now, however, Sarge noticed us in the cells. If he could shatter that cylinder—and he did— then there was a very good probability that he could shatter our doors as well. He stomped toward our wall and punched out the first cage's transparent aluminium door. I could hear it rumble through the underground facility's entire structure. Then the second, then the third, and on and on until he came to my cage, the final one. I ducked and covered as his huge fist rammed into the door and reduced it to shards.

He couldn't talk—he was a Gray, somehow he had been turned instantly into the biggest and fiercest Gray we had yet seen—but he motioned for us all to follow him over to the lab seating and rest for a moment. Leonard, Junebug, Inman, Hog, Gunner, Fugly, Ernie, Calico all hugged and bumped fists and everything else to celebrate that we were alive, that Sarge had kept us alive and now saved us …

Someone chuckled. It turned into a laugh, and then a series of guffaws that lasted until his breath ran out. Then the laughing started again with a new intake of breath. Those looking in Sarge's direction froze in place, and the rest of us turned around … and also froze in place.

Where the Stage 2 twelve-foot super-soldier War Thug had been, now laughing was one of the Stage 1 waxen-looking Yellows. One with Sarge's face, crying with laughter.

In a few more minutes, our commander was able to get a hold of himself, having returned to his original size and coloring. He had become human again. Naked again as well, but we'd all seen each other in the buff a million times in the close confines of the *Blue Celeste*. He found his uniform on the floor, not too much the worse for wear considering how he treated them in the first place, and put it back on. It didn't quite fit anymore—this massive man, after becoming a twelve-foot monster, hadn't quite returned to his normal size. He was even bigger. But he was all Sarge.

"Gather 'round, boys and girls, it's story time."

With smiles, despite all the blood and gore around us, we stood around the lab table Sarge had picked, the table with his torn-off automail mechanical arm on it.

"Because of that big-mouthed bitch, you all know that my War Council Enhancement is *targeted rage*. When I see Xenos to kill, my mind becomes clear, clear like the waters of Earth."

Terra? Why did he say Earth? Us grunts exchanged glances, but that was all.

He continued: "I become clear and focused on ending every potential terrorist bug or sentient I see. I wondered if this might happen, but when they put me in that contraption and filled me with their fine-tuned frequency radiation, what got excited was the part of my glandular system Enhanced with that *rage*."

"*Everyone reacts a little differently to the initial dose*," I said, quoting the late Doctor Ripple.

"That's right," Sarge said. "My exact Enhancement got Enhanced in a way they didn't expect—it just exploded. I shot up to the highest Stage 2, but because what was Enhanced was *targeted rage*, I killed all of them—and only them, none of you—before the first dose's effects wore off and I dwindled back down to my usual petite self."

He made us snicker, but then turned stone serious in an instant.

"According to the whitecoats over there, the entirety of Planet Bunghole is populated by Yellows and Grays, former Space Navy

SEALs reduced to brute animals who can only follow orders. Now they have no one to order them, ever, and so they'll wander this planet until the War Council gets wise and comes to get them. They are slaves. Right now they're free in one sense, but they will be slaves of the Council before too long."

"Sarge, we can't scour the whole planet to kill every one of these luckless bastards," Inman said. "Besides, when the War Council sees the automatically transmitted vidlogs of this whole affair, they'll execute us in front of every man, woman, and child on Terra. We went rogue. We're mutineers now, sir."

Our boss nodded at Inman. "That's true, but don't forget that the Council has a way of forgetting, if not forgiving, missteps by its personnel. They'll run you out of the force, put you to work in the spice mines of Kessel or whatnot, but there isn't more than one public execution of a platoon each week."

"That sounds delightful, sir," Fugly said with a gallows-humor smirk.

We all looked dejected. I know I did. But then Sarge gave the table a little pound with his fist, and instantly our attention was on him again. "Listen, men, *targeted rage* isn't my only Enhancement."

Exclamations of surprise and disbelief arose around the table. "Sir, I'm very sorry to contradict you," I said, "but I can't recall a single published case in which an individual has ever exhibited more than one Enhanced ability."

"True, Boswell, very true. Maybe I shouldn't call it an Enhancement, really." He picked up his prosthetic arm. Automail was expensive as anything the service would pay for, and wouldn't pay for it twice. "Tell you what: let's get to the drop site and I'll tell you my juiciest secret. Also, Ace must be worried as hell about us poor chickens down here. Ernie, can you hail the ship?"

"Aye, sir. Ace says she's ready when we're ready. And also, she's glad we're alive."

"Hell, I would *hope* she is," Sarge said with a laugh, and very carefully ninja-moved out the lab door, through the curving hallway, and one by one up the rungs that led to what was left of the gazebo.

We made it up and onto the wooden floor, our beautiful Space Elevator cable fifty yards away. The Yellows and Grays were nowhere to be seen, apparently keeping their distance even if they did see us.

"Troops, this planet is an abomination of everything that every branch of the Council Space Military stands for. It's slavery of our own people. That same War Council has destroyed and ended the lives of uncountable SEALs who came here on what they thought was a mission of mercy. But it was a trap.

"None of these poor sons of bitches even remember they were Space Navy SEALs or with what bravery they served. They will all starve to death here, or they'll be picked up by Council carriers to extend their suffering on moons and planets as long as they live, which could be centuries for all we know."

"So what do we do about it, sir?" Calico said.

"My second Enhancement," Sarge said as he held up his mechanized arm. "Inside this automail prosthetic, my friends, is a Super-Nuke."

Jaws dropped. Eyes goggled with shock. We all leaned in even as we wanted to get as far away from it as possible.

"When I was a grunt like you guys, a Thermian octoscorp got me cornered and wrapped its tentacle around my arm and squeezed. It cut right through me like razor wire. I was lucky I had the railgun in the other hand, blasted that bastard into atoms.

"But the medics got me and I was transported to the closest med-base in the quadrant. After I regained consciousness, the War

Council bigwigs visited me in sick bay and told me I would finally get my own platoon if I … well, if I would allow myself to be a human doomsday weapon. The Super-Nuke was installed in the arm, the mechanical arm was attached to me, and if I ever got the order to basically *erase* every living thing from megafauna to bacteria—not to mention eat away every topological feature from oceans to mountains on a particular gone-FUBAR planet—I was to execute that order immediately.

"That's the story, folks. And this right here is a Super-Nuke." He placed it on the ground.

"Sir, if I may ask, why are you telling us about this now?" Hog said.

"I don't want to let these brave men and women—*former*, maybe, but still—die slowly and without dignity. And I don't want the War Council ever to use this super-Enhancement technology ever again."

"You want to Super-Nuke this entire planet," Inman said. "If we do that, sir, we'll be wanted as traitors and criminals throughout the inhabited galaxy."

"We got food-growing materials up there, ramjet fuel collection, water creators, everything we need to be self-sufficient indefinitely. But I won't do it without a vote. Boswell?"

"All in favor of becoming intergalactic super-criminals who fight the War Council at every turn for the rest of their natural-born lives, raise your hand," I said, getting a smile from everyone including Sarge. Every single SEAL's arm went up. "I vote *yea* as well. We're with you, Sarge."

He was happy and proud, everyone could see that. "Boswell, stay with me. Everybody else, get your gear on and your asses clipped in proper order on the elevator cable, double-time," he said. He had me hold the metal arm while he punched in a series of codes. "All right, we got sixty seconds from … *now*."

I placed the Super-Nuke on the ground and ran for the Space Elevator, fiddling with the pressure suit I grabbed from the supply compartment at the base of the cable. As always, Sarge clipped on last. "Why don't we just do this from orbit?" Killshot said just before Ace started reeling us up, and *fast*.

"We gotta nuke 'em from the surface. It's the only way to be sure," Sarge said, and we were hauled into the sky so fast that most of us lost consciousness for a moment somewhere along the way from blood rushing away from our brains.

When we were about midway between Planet Bunghole and the *Blue Celeste*, the Super-Nuke exploded. We couldn't hear anything in the emptiness of space, but we could see the shock waves from the detonation spread out across the surface, burning everything, killing everything including those poor SEALs who didn't have Sarge for their platoon commander. I saluted them. Later, I was told that everyone did.

***

"Subspace transmission coming in from Terran Command, sir," Ace said to Sarge, leading all of us to look quizzically at Ernie, who normally would be the gateway for electronic transmissions.

"Light us up back here," Sarge said, and the vidscreen showed Admiral Hollister, head of Space Navy operations. Sitting next to him was Secretary Kelloway, head of the War Council and so essentially the president-for-life of Planet Earth. Both men were livid with rage, but Kelloway stared into the vidcam like a snake; Admiral Hollister shook with rage as he spoke.

"*Blue Celeste*, we have never before experienced such traitorous actions as those reported to Space Navy Command by your logman," the Admiral practically spat. No one even bothered looking at me funny; Sarge told me to put together an absolutely accurate account, one that explained why the final action on L-22233 was taken. There was no sense in lying, anyway—our platoon was supposed to be the cherry on top of this new super-soldier Enhancement operation, so the Council would know what had happened before too long anyway. "You have single-handedly ruined *years* of military research and investment. Not only did you bring to an ignominious end the dreams of a better and stronger anti-terrorism military, but you murdered thousands of SEALs, dedicated men and women who wanted only to make Earth a safer homeland. You—"

"Allow me to add my two cents, if I may, Admiral," Kelloway said, his icy tone a counterpoint to Hollister's hot anger. "We are going to hunt you down, War Thug, you and your accomplices. If you go to any Council base, any resort planet, any known supply hubs, we will know. We will find you and we will destroy you. If we can, we will take you alive so that you may be introduced to the finest interrogation techniques ever developed. It will take a long time for you to die."

"So are we Enemies of the State?" Sarge asked, bemused.

"You'd better believe you are, you musclebound tub of—"

"Then this is *war*, Mister Secretary. The War Council is our enemy now. The captain and crew of the *Blue Celeste* are going to fight you anywhere and everywhere we go. "

Kelloway scoffed. "Do you really think you can win this battle?"

"Who knows? But we ain't lost one yet."

The End

CHECK OUT OTHER GREAT SCIENCE FICTION BOOKS

MAUSOLEUM 2069
by Rick Jones

Political dignitaries including the President of the Federation gather for a ceremony onboard Mausoleum 2069. But when a cloud of interstellar dust passes through the galaxy and eclipses Earth, the tenants within the walls of Mausoleum 2069 are reborn and the undead begin to rise. As the struggle between life and death onboard the mausoleum develops, Eriq Wyman, a one-time member of a Special ops team called the Force Elite, is given the task to lead the President to the safety of Earth. But is Earth like Mausoleum 2069? A landscape of the living dead? Has the war of the Apocalypse finally begun? With so many questions there is only one certainty: in space there is nowhere to run and nowhere to hide.

RED CARBON
by D.J. Goodman

Diamonds have been discovered on Mars.

After years of neglect to space programs around the world, a ruthless corporation has made it to the Red Planet first, establishing their own mining operation with its own rules and laws, its own class system, and little oversight from Earth. Conditions are harsh, but its people have learned how to make the Martian colony home.

But something has gone catastrophically wrong on Earth. As the colony leaders try to cover it up, hacker Leah Hartnup is getting suspicious. Her boundless curiosity will lead her to a horrifying truth: they are cut off, possibly forever. There are no more supplies coming. There will be no more support. There is no more mission to accomplish. All that's left is one goal: survival.

CHECK OUT OTHER GREAT SCIENCE FICTION BOOKS

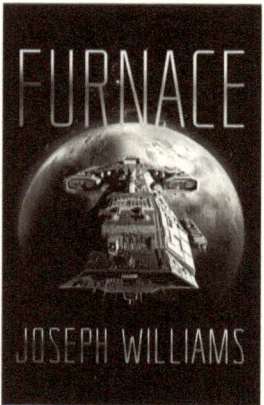

FURNACE
by Joseph Williams

On a routine escort mission to a human colony, Lieutenant Michael Chalmers is pulled out of hyper-sleep a month early. The RSA Rockne Hummel is well off course and—as the ship's navigator—it's up to him to figure out why. It's supposed to be a simple fix, but when he attempts to identify their position in the known universe, nothing registers on his scans. The vessel has catapulted beyond the reach of starlight by at least a hundred trillion light-years. Then a planetary-mass object materializes behind them. It's burning brightly even without a star to heat it. Hundreds of damaged ships are locked in its orbit. The crew discovers there are no life-signs aboard any of them. As system failures sweep through the Hummel, neither Chalmers nor the pilot can prevent the vessel from crashing into the surface near a mysterious ancient city. And that's where the real nightmare begins.

LUNA
by Rick Chesler

On the threshold of opening the moon to tourist excursions, a private space firm owned by a visionary billionaire takes a team of non-astronauts to the lunar surface. To address concerns that the moon's barren rock may not hold long-term allure for an uber-wealthy clientele, the company's charismatic owner reveals to the group the ultimate discovery: life on the moon.

But what is initially a triumphant and world-changing moment soon gives way to unrelenting terror as the team experiences firsthand that despite their technological prowess, the moon still holds many secrets.

CHECK OUT OTHER GREAT SCIENCE FICTION BOOKS

IN PERPETUITY
by Jake Bible

For two thousand years, Earth and her many colonies across the galaxy have fought against the Estelian menace. Having faced overwhelming losses, the CSC has instituted the largest military draft ever, conscripting millions into the battle against the aliens. Major Bartram North has been tasked with the unenviable task of coordinating the military education of hundreds of thousands of recruits and turning them into troops ready to fight and die for the cause.

As Major North struggles to maintain a training pace that the CSC insists upon, he realizes something isn't right on the Perpetuity. But before he can investigate, the station dissolves into madness brought on by the physical booster known as pharma. Unfortunately for Major North, that is not the only nightmare he faces- an armada of Estelian warships is on the edge of the solar system and headed right for Earth!

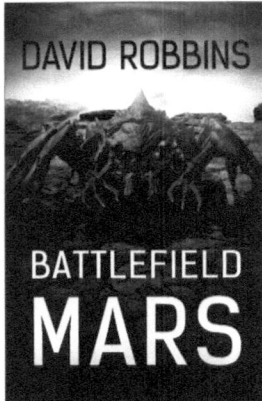

BATTLEFIELD MARS
by David Robbins

Several centuries into the future, Earth has established three colonies on Mars. No indigenous life has been discovered, and humankind looks forward to making the Red Planet their own.

Then 'something' emerges out of a long-extinct volcano and doesn't like what the humans are doing.

Captain Archard Rahn, United Nations Interplanetary Corps, tries to stem the rising tide of slaughter. But the Martians are more than they seem, and it isn't long before Mars erupts in all-out war.

CHECK OUT OTHER GREAT SCIENCE FICTION BOOKS

SALVAGE MERC ONE
by **Jake Bible**

Joseph Laribeau was born to be a Marine in the Galactic Fleet. He was born to fight the alien enemies known as the Skrang Alliance and travel the galaxy doing his duty as a Marine Sergeant. But when the War ended and Joe found himself medically discharged, the best job ever was over and he never thought he'd find his way again.

Then a beautiful alien walked into his life and offered him a chance at something even greater than the Fleet, a chance to serve with the Salvage Merc Corp.

Now known as Salvage Merc One Eighty-Four, Joe Laribeau is given the ultimate assignment by the SMC bosses. To his surprise it is neither a military nor a corporate salvage. Rather, Joe has to risk his life for one of his own. He has to find and bring back the legend that started the Corp.

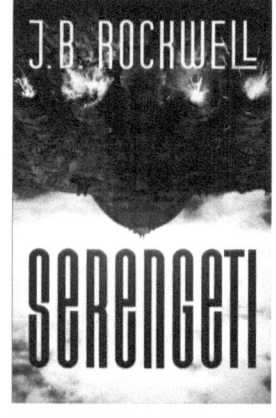

SERENGETI
by **J.B. Rockwell**

It was supposed to be an easy job: find the Dark Star Revolution Starships, destroy them, and go home. But a booby-trapped vessel decimates the Meridian Alliance fleet, leaving Serengeti—a Valkyrie class warship with a sentient AI brain—on her own; wrecked and abandoned in an empty expanse of space. On the edge of total failure, Serengeti thinks only of her crew. She herds the survivors into a lifeboat, intending to sling them into space. But the escape pod sticks in her belly, locking the cryogenically frozen crew inside.

Then a scavenger ship arrives to pick Serengeti's bones clean. Her engines dead, her guns long silenced, Serengeti and her last two robots must find a way to fight the scavengers off and save the crew trapped inside her.

www.ingramcontent.com/pod-product-compliance
Lightning Source LLC
Chambersburg PA
CBHW030533130626
46552CB00006B/2234